Beautiful

A Poetic Celebration
of Displaced Children

Beautiful

A Poetic Celebration
of Displaced Children

Jaiya John

SW❀R

Soul Water Rising

Ojai, California

Soul Water Rising
Ojai, California
http://www.soulwater.org

Library of Congress Control Number: 2013921730
ISBN 978-0-9916401-1-9

Second Soul Water Rising Edition, Softcover: 2014

Poetry / Spoken Word / Child & Youth Development

Editors:
Jacqueline V. Richmond
Charlene R. Maxwell
Kent W. Mortensen

Cover Artwork: Eddye "Adiya"
Cover & Interior Design: Jaiya John

for our young melodies
yearning to become eternal song

AUTHOR'S NOTE

This second edition of *Beautiful* contains eight new pieces that I hope will add richness, meaning, and enjoyment to your experience with the book. Also, this new edition's book cover jacket has been blessed by the artwork of Eddye "Adiya." Her own life journey mirrors that of many of the stories in *Beautiful*. I cannot envision someone more providential to convey the spirit of this book. I am grateful.

This poetry is a continuous river of vibrant tears, washing over life's sediment to reveal the shimmering beauty of our uprooted young. Some beauty is hidden beneath youthful blemish. Some beauty stands clear before us. Our challenge is to *see* this radiance. Our young are purpose-full. Beautiful is their *name*.

    Beautiful is a poetic companion to the nonfiction book *Reflection Pond: Seeing the Sacred in Displaced Children*. Like *Reflection Pond*, *Beautiful* brings us nearer to youth who have been separated from their original families. Here, young voices encountered in my life's work are rendered in fictional poetry and poetic stories inspired by their sheer human luminosity. I wrote these poems for both youth and adults, intending to transmit the honest, unobstructed spirit of children.

Our young are often burdened with categories and labels we assign them. So too is poetry. For this reason, although titles have been added to this second edition, I have allowed these poems and stories to range free, without categories, or sections. Please discover them in your own personal way.

I wrote many of these poems as part of my speaking engagements through the years—they are longer and contain rhythm, rhyme, and language designed for narrative messaging and dramatic effect. Such *performance poems* were intended for audiences who were without the advantage of digesting words from the page at their own pace. Other poems in *Beautiful* are more contemplative, concise.

Some poetry is best eaten raw, for the listening soul. Some is best served cooked, for the reader apt to linger on the verbal imagery. *Beautiful* contains a gumbo of such poetic types, all leading to a central truth: Childhood separation reveals our human vulnerability and our human majesty.

MIRACLE'S FACE

This world calls us:

at risk, troubled, tainted, homeless, orphan, abused, abandoned, violated, neglected, angry, oppositional, disabled, special needs, violent, bad, rotten, dysfunctional, abnormal, truant, traumatized, impoverished, delinquent, drop-out, damaged goods, unworthy, unwanted, unable, hopeless, placeless, faceless...

We say *this* to the world:

You brand me with words like cattle. I am the canvas for your foul imagination. How do I know this? I read your mind a thousand times. The easy children get your valentines. I get your lemon rinds. But right here, right now, it's miracle time. I'm becoming what you said I would never be. Legacy. History. Sanctity.

How do I know this?
because I blow this... false idea of me
into a flame of Truth

and it's not too late for you to renovate,
realize you were wrong about me...
just write a new song about me,
revise your notes, erase your vision,
choose new paint... inferior?
I ain't that worthless taint,

I'm a different kind of saint,
I'm the brand that keeps
whacking down the jungle vines
even as they swarm my throat,
the kind that crosses the burning moat,
the kind that keeps on Loving even as you hate,
keeps on rising even as you keep on steppin

I'm a keeper, I keep on,
I hold on till dawn,
got my Truth eyes on,
pawn my smile just to get your respect,
sell my privacy to whistle blow
what you say about me, think about me,
read about me, right now we're gonna
dead this lie about me, get down in the dirt
and pray about me, have a better say about me

I ball my fist, tense my wrist,
kiss the lips of your prejudice,
give your blindness a black eye,
open up your mental sky

you pour salt into my rain,
I work steady to heal my pain,
I resolve to beautify my attitude,
you drop a drive-by, blasting labels
and rumors at me from your
sawed off sensitivity

here's a tip:
when you reach my street, don't fly by,
slow your roll, stop your thought cop'n,
your eyes are poppin, you see a monster,
but monsters made my childhood bed,

now I'm tossin the sheets, flippin my
circumstance, changing channels on my dreams

I refuse to be a stigma... enigma is: I'm greater
than my challenges, bigger than my barricades,
don't give up on me, I'm a lantern lifting
in the Sky of Hope, I'm an avalanche of change
moving down the slope

I metamorphosis, I was *made* for this, I'm the
morning mist, evidence of a frigid night,
evaporating into sunlight's clarity, that brilliant
rarity, I BE the sweeter tea, epiphany, symphony

you never saw me coming, now I'm sacred
drumming, communing with my ancestors,
learning languages great ones speak, you see me
meek, I see blessing in the valley creek, I see
mountains rising, trees talking about my soul

life gives me pressure, I become a pearl,
I transformer, spirit reformer, former stormer,
now the Calm... I am the silence when you pray,
the echo of your childhood, the temple sound

all false words touch my Truth fire,
burn to the ground,
I AM living, breathing Grace,
I AM the infinite flame
in the human fireplace

Creation is a miracle

I AM its face.

I LEAD MYSELF

I wake this day
and kneel and pray

my entire life, all the joy and strife,
rises at my inner shore

I have momentary solid,
now I want more

stigma unfurls its dreadful wings
and shadows me, cold predator

labels and categories move to pen me up

I ain't no penitentiary pup,
I'm not giving up

so I kneel and pray,
open up my soul-jer chest,
reach this hand down into *my* life,
pull up something raw and fresh

I smoke this, toke this, invoke this Peace

not blunt but bliss, all suffering cease

I breathe an air so rare, not a tear to spare,
I've been to there, now I care to share
the dare to be a better I

Sun climbs sky, sits on its blue shelf

I turn inside and look to self,
I reckon with what I see in the glass:
my past, my present, what comes
to walk with me

I know I can't do this life like a champion
unless I bless I, train like a legend

so I, I lead myself

I lead myself to Truth,
track scent of my own Holy water

I lead myself to Greatness born in me

I lead myself to Integrity,
land of milk and honey,
fertilized by Clarity

I lead myself to Inspiration, Creativity,
I make new life, new family, new world

I lead myself to the Light,
spin webs of mental positivity

I lead myself to Power,
translating my pain into motivation,
find courage to forgive,
so I won't be a slave to anger,
won't be a prostitute to pain,
won't be a pimp running gangs
of manipulation, won't flip tricks,
won't sip sick liquids,

won't stick poison in my veins,
won't remain soaking in purple rain,
won't sex my way down the drain,
won't prove the lie that my kind
are born to die, won't slide by,
step over, pretend not to see
when my broken brother need me,
when my beat down sister bleed, see

I lead myself to pure devotion,
swimming ocean after ocean
of life's commotion to reach
calmer waters, calm my future sons,
calm my one day daughters

I dive deep into the soul of me,
searching for the hole in me,
the one my circumstance
bore in me, so I can mend
the wound, seal the sore in me

see, the floor in me is not the roof,
I can't live upside down,
acting hard, but being nothing
but a punk drunk clown

so I dive deep into the soul of me,
scrape my comfort against coral reef

I've got no beef with Paradise,
just having trouble finding it

I need new GPS,
so I download a premium app
called Leadership,

accept the terms and policies...
now I'm rolling, trolling days
with net cast crazy ways,
not gonna be the place
where crazy stays,
where crazy lays

hands deep in clay,
shaping my life from masquerade
to grand parade,
squeezing my Truth,
gathering vital juice,
making ice cold lemonade,
my worries fade
as I drink sweetness down,
I profound, I the sound
of sacred coming round

I lead myself to this inner bliss,
this Forever Peace,
this social movement to free
my kind from hopelessness,
I swing the rope of this
life of mine made from sacred vine,
I valentine my dreams and visions,
I invite my Passion to dance,
I romance what *I* want *my* life to be,
I seduce the blues in me to change
their tune, to shine like hip hop moon

I lead myself,
I become the legendary Leader Ship
that sails from dock of despair
over transformation waters
on a course for Dream-I-Born-Ya,

dream I warn ya, dream I storm ya,
dream I form ya into a brand new land

I lead myself,
I bleed myself of all my toxins,
I purify my mental sky,
I burn clear flame for service to souls in need,
I advocate, I never too late,
I miracle worker, I field hand
standing hand in hand
with my brothers and sisters
who harvest the sweeter fruit

I Leader Ship,
unsinkable, unsayable,
unbelievable, unbreakable,
cutting waves, freeing slaves,
carrying courageous cargo

I know how far I go,
I go how far I say I go,
not how far this world decides,
I doe ray me doe, I flow

I release myself,
I police myself,
I bless myself,
unstress myself,
undress my lesser self,
reveal my Higher self

I... LEAD... MY... SELF.

THIS HOME I AM

The job interview takes place over lunch...

employer says to the teenager:

so, I've notice your résumé appears a little thin,
please share with me what you feel your value is

teenager wipes his mouth, takes a drink of water,
beads falling down the glass
as beads trace down his face

composing himself with the thought of
a cloudless peaceful sky,
he begins to unravel the spool of his life,
the answer to all his questions *why*

he says: ... I know how to live

excuse me?

I said, I know how to live

I know how to scavenge birdseed from parks and
stuff my pocket with bread crust from trash bins

I know what time at night is safest to pillage dog
food from saucers in green backyards
and cat food from gray tins

I know which spot under the bridge

doesn't carry too much wind
so I can wake in the morning
not drenched or frozen

I know I am not the chosen...
but I know how to choose my friends

people can use the word *friend* like a Trojan horse,
wanting you to let down your guard
so they can get close to you
and do the damage a friend would never do

I know how to choose my friends

I know how to recognize my father on the street
in his tattered raincoat and his stench and stupor,
and I know enough to Love him even though we
never played ball or went fishing or talked or took
walks or ate dinner at the table

I know enough to know my father's pain runs like
maple in the cold of fall, and even though he has
been consumed by it, my father *is not his pain*,
it is his prison but it is not him

he is a little lost boy, walking the streets of his
trauma, a monk who prays in confusion,
meditates on madness, and fills his beggar's bowl
with the strangest grain of rice

I know enough to recognize my father
and still pray he finds his paradise

I know enough to recognize my mother
when she comes to me in dreams,

sometimes she is a valley filled with trees of fruit,
sometimes a bright lagoon
with tears of joy waterfalling down

sometimes she is a clown, trying her best to cheer
me up, even though a perfect life
stayed miles away from her

still, she served me perfect meals of grace
and the peace of knowing she never tried to hurt
me with knifing words or hateful face

I know how to recognize my mother
when she comes to me in dreams

I know what to do when
people look at me and imagine nothingness,
I just remember who I am, and that I was born
to walk this road and keep on walking until
the stones turn into serenity, and my feet no
longer touch the ground, because I myself have
become true light, a force of will and nature
who has figured out the purpose to his plight

I know when to catch the tears of a stranger
when they're falling in a certain way down her
weary face... I know Grace

and I know how to express my life to you:

homeless, ocean foamless, I moan this poem,
this aloneness, cactus plains I roam this,
awesome ache I own this

I fill my lake of soul with song and stone this...
water, rippling my ownness to shore to touch my
soul sound against the toneless

lying on earth at night
I stare at my promise sky so domeless

I strike the flint of pain against my existence
to start a fire so I can hone this groan,
this bone I've known
that others gnaw at like a rabid rat,
this name by which I'm known,
this stigma that claws me like caged up cat,
this boiling vat pouring molten emotion
into the air I breathe,
this shame that floods me, my soul a sieve,
the world that dogs me of my joy,
the persistent daily thieve

but I do exist and so I grieve, I grieve,
you best believe that when you leave
I return to what *I* believe

see *sometimes I feel like a motherless child*
and *sometimes I feel so fatherless, child,*
and sometimes I turn to the void and ask:
how come me here?

and sometimes I sing:
I wish I never was born...
and as I sing, new life is born inside my
mountain spring, my valley stream

and I realize I was born with
fierce drumbeat inside my chest

powerful enough to part the skies

and as long as I locate my beat and remain,
no matter how long the rain or deep the pain,
or absent the sane from my life and grain,
as long as I hold onto my sacred beat
and determine to be true to I,
then *wherever* I journey in this world,
I am home and kiss the sky

I may come to have a home of wood and stone,
but if I am not true to I,
that touchable home may as well not exist,
for if I am not true to this innerness,
then all around me is less than mist

but if I find I, and honor I,
then I am truly home, home inside my truth,
home inside any relationship, home in any place,
on any road, in any moment, in every
circumstance

one romance feeds all the rest:
I must Love I enough to move
into the one home that can never crumble,
I must sign the unbreakable lease
written on the brilliant page of Peace,
I must reside in the one place made for I,
whose windows are always filled with light & sky

what do I know?
I know how to do what most others have never
done: lie in darkness and stroke the sun

it takes free fall through fate to learn to fly,

and the choke of bitter nakedness
to cherish the pristine taste of bliss,
I do know *this*

what do I know?
I know how to own this, homeless roam,
this momentary, secondary space
that looks to have no floor,
this room that seems to have no door

I know how to create that floor,
construct that freedom door,
move from shadows into light,
and make this life my home

I know how to recite this poem I am,
ignite this light I am,
invite this flight I am,
breathe peace, spread roots,
grow stalks of Love,
cook meals of soul and sound,
sleep deep in silence,
wake fresh, bathe clean,
open windows to the wonder of life
and live
and live
inside
this home
I am.

YOUNG LIFE NEEDS MUSIC

Young life needs *music*,
so young life closes eyes,
heartbeat on the rise,
takes a deep breath,
lets out all the grown folk sound,
so young life can dig deep and get on down

here it come, the sound of drum

here it come, *ba rum pa pum pum*

young life says: *listen to my drum...*

listen to my lyric
as I walk solo through
the jungle of my life for you

soul machete at the ready,
cutting down all the profound jungle sound
that keeps on keeping me down

all the vines, they keep reminding me
of all the times
someone didn't want me to learn
what it means to be free

didn't want me to have a choice,
didn't want to hear my voice

so now I muster up the courage

to walk from darkness into light

downloading sun beams
till I get my music right,
till I get my tunes real tight

then I'm gonna drop the album of my life
and set all the haters straight

see, to know who I truly am,
you gotta listen to my drumbeat, man

I'm banging with my music 'cause
my music never lets me down

I'm building bridges
with my cool beats
so I can walk out
from the steady pain rain
over troubled waters
and find my amazing grace,
my peace place

so I can
kneel down into my reflection
and finally see my true face

see, you two-faced
when you start talking 'bout
my proper place,
then you lead me by the hand
straight into quicksand

come on, my man,
drop the false hand

and listen to my *music,*
feel my song

it's trying to tell you
how to help me help *myself*

all you gotta do
is stop trying to stigmatize,
stop telling lies and *google* me

look up my genuine record
of young life foolery

you'll see that each time I stumbled,
underground, my earth rumbled,
my sense of safety crumbled

can't you see?
I don't need to be humbled,
I need to be lifted up

don't wanna be a slave no more,
don't wanna be chained to fear,
trying to keep my drumbeat near,
trying to dance in my given dust

you keep pulling out the carpet
from beneath my battered trust

I'm tired of hurting my soul brother,
tired of putting down my soul sister,
hey mister, hey ma'am,
can you please show me where I am?

I got lost in your world,

now I walk through the jungle
playing deceitful songs in my head

vines wrapping 'round my neck,
vultures see my jeopardy,
so now they come to peck

strangers rolling up on me,
all of them saying, *follow me!*

none saying, *hey there young,*
can I follow you?
can you show me where your heart goes
when it's steady fleeing foes,
when your instinct knows
something's coming,
a hidden thorn beneath the rose

can you show me, young
what it takes to get you drumming?
what's the music that leaves you humming?

see I, young life be, I free,
and I want the grown ones
to holster their authority guns
and seek the greatness inside of me

my young life has simple needs:
when my heart is blessed, it shines,
when it's cut, it bleeds

excuse me, mister/ma'am authority,
one who's supposed to be
steady looking out for me,
can I respectfully ask you something?

can you please go online and *download me?*

not my outer imperfection,
but my greatest hits remix,
the one that sounds like
young life resurrection

download the album of my life,
put me on replay, sit back, smile
and soak me up

let's make crazy music together

my heart chest feels restless breathless weariness,
something fearless stirs though, deep inside

here... come close to me,
can you feel my drumbeat coming?
can you hear my promise humming?

kneel down on this humble ground between us

don't come at me,
be with me

put your sacred soul hand
on my holy drum land
and beat some truth with me

let's make crazy music
and set each other way past free.

I CHOOSE TO BE ME

I'm that young one
with the muzzled tongue,
my heart bruised and stung
by a ton of bees
buzzing through my harmonies,
thinking they're my enemies

I wanna say please, please,
I'm not a disease,
I'm just like the trees
bending in the ocean breeze

so please, please,
get down on your humble knees
and look up at the sky,
I'm that shy bird flying by,
dropping silent tears as rain as I fly high

I'm not the sour stain,
I'm just the rain
releasing my pain
in fat drops, pops

and I hate to burst your bubble
but I'm not the trouble,
I'm the light that trouble chases,
I'm all the places your fear won't let you go...
hear me though:

I'm not the flat note,

I'm the tune that's steady playing,
steady prayin that you'll hear me yo

but you ain't hearing me,
you've got other places to go,
seeds to sow,
normal faces to polish,
dreams like mine to demolish

and that's all right,
cause I was born with a sacred vision,
all your doubts can't take me from my mission

my life isn't a perfect one
but the light inside me is still perfect son,
my silence has had its run,
now it's time to beat my drum,
release my sun,
drop my number one

I'm that volcano that you label
even though I'm a volcano you don't know

my stuff's been brewin like molten lava
deep in my life soil,
now it's rising fast, on the boil,
I'm getting ready-set-go to show
all that I truly am

I'm about to paint this world
in the truth I see,
I'm gonna tell a new kind of story,
one that brings dark to light
and frees young souls like me
to be a kite in flight,

shining peace in every corner of the night

I'm gonna plant a seed of faith in myself
and reap a heap of courage and belief

I'm gonna walk tall and straight
and let the haters hate,
I've got another fate,
one that starts in struggle
and ends in Great

I once was blind but now I see,
I was born with a song
so I'm gonna sing it

I was born with a gift
so I'm gonna bring it

I was born to be exactly who I be,
so I choose to *use* my pain
and shatter my chain

I choose to be free
I choose
I choose
I *choose*... to be... *ME.*

WHEN I OPEN UP MY BOOK

When I open up my book... look,
come and see my lesson plan,
come and see my vision, man

when I open up my brain, pain
comes running through my mainframe,
downloading viruses to my main game

day after day the same pain,
keeping me from hearing my true name,
so I had to claim my pain,
make it bow down and serve my mission,
now that same pain is steady fishin
for the greatness in my mission
and I can hear my true name...
it starts with: *no one to blame*,
goes on to: *nothing can stop my game*,
ends with: *every day I'm gonna bring
a new rain... down on my heart,
make all this confusion plain*

gonna change the world with what I learn
about the purpose of my sorrow stain,
my joy train, my triumph on the path I walk,
the flowin creak of knowledge
that I follow all the way to college,
and from there I dare to keep on drinkin'
from the fountain of my youth,
keep on learnin life in all its truth,
keep on openin up my soul, Joe,

see, my final goal is to use my education
to change my struggle in the valley
to a lifetime livin at a higher elevation,
to straight revolutionize this nation

and for my final cup of tea,
to touch humanity, and set it clear and free,
so young ones like me, will believe they can,
write a better lesson plan, better than another
ever can... for a young one who's walking
a crazy road, carryin a crazy load

so when I open up my book... look,
come and see my lesson plan,
come and see my vision, man...

when I open up my book...

MY HOUR COMES AT LAST

18 years passin through the hourglass,
now my hour comes at last

like a sea turtle, I've come from the cracked
egg shell of my imperfect life, and perfectly
I've followed instinct to reach the sea,
where I have this opportunity,
to live my life independently

like that turtle hatchling,
I've crossed the endless sand grains
of joys and pains,
and now I've reached my ocean wide,
my chance to walk the ocean side,
open up my hidden inner side,
and let the beauty of relationship,
moving toward me like an ocean ship,
catch the wave of my curiosity,
and riding on the ocean tide,
wash over me and bless my tenderness
with the ointment of epiphany,
which can only come to me
through an awesome Love affair
with the human world out there

an awesome Love affair, that's mine only if I dare
to fall in Love with life and learning, cause a life
of learning can bring satisfaction to my yearning,
and lifelong education can open me and help to let
the hurtin go, and let my joy come in

so today I graduate from where I've been,
and pick up new eyes to see the greatness my life
has put in me, all my endless possibility
is right here with me

all I have to do to truly end my dependency
and cross the graduation stage, is learn to Love
learning, and Love to learn Loving

cause Love and learning, will unearth my passion
burning, and bring me to my purpose, and open
up my giftedness, wrapped up in my tenderness

so now I choose to read and write
the story of MY life,
which starts in struggle and ends in Peace,
and finds me walkin by my ocean side,
embracing change brought by ocean tide

18 years passin through the hourglass,
now my hour comes at last, I choose to use my
past to change my identity, so I can change the
world that lives inside of me

I choose to use my fate,
I choose to make my goodness great,
I choose to graduate, to cross my stage
and open up the book of life,
reading page to page and never stopping

so I say to all of you,
thank goodness for my past,
cause now my hour comes at last.

GRADUATION DAY

She, on this day,
valedictorian, *worthy speaker,*
rises and steps poised to the podium

no notes

only a long rehearsed expression of yearning
for people not present in flesh,
a circle of intimacy she has not seen
in 36 seasons on earth:

Good morning ladies and gentlemen...
on this bright and honorable morning
I would like to ask you to excuse me
as I first address some people
who are not able to be here with us

I am hopeful that you will take my message
to them as a message to all...

clearing the nerves from her throat and shooing
the butterflies from her stomach, she begins:

To my dear family...

on this, my graduation day, I want to let you
know how much you have meant to me, even
though I have not seen you in nine years

memories of you are the sweet blood
that runs through my happiness

the nectar that makes possible my sorrow

I have furrows in my character
that your investment entrenched in plentiful rows

my melancholy now, speaks of a great joy then

for achievement is what remains
after easy things are boiled away

the scent of you opens the blossom of my heart

dreams of you bring me back to the shores
of my belonging, sturdy me once more
for my long swim across this lake of life

stories we shared, now gone to dust, became seed
and sprouted into morals and values that carry me

our Love cannot be eclipsed by time or distance,
cannot be eroded by tears or tragedy,
cannot be placated so easily as to say,
we were family once

nothing is enough, short of saying,
we are family still

together we cross this graduation stage

together our spirits matriculate through
seasons of living, ascend ladders of purpose
to reach a mystical lake where only those who
have been Loved may bow and drink a water of
abundance without end.

SILENT DESIRES

Ease me

I am that place where river meets rock
and becomes white water

I am that place of transformation and foam

I need a tide pool,
I need a home

full moon preens
to its own beauty
basking on mirror surface
of placid waters

the child I am is envy swollen,
I cast a stone and break
that reflection with ripples
silent and hurried,
like the desires,
wet and unwelcome,
that litter my shore.

RIVER STONE

An adolescent ponders belongingness:

I wish I was the river

now, I am the river stone...

cold water diamond clear
rushes over me, life flows past,
drowning me in its eternity

my shape is polished by faithful current...
if I breathe deeply, open my pores,
my spirit too is polished in this endless bath

trees shade me from sky above,
scattering dark across water,
like leaves sent to scurry over...
no point other than the intimacy of touching

memories reach me from their source upstream,
my sediment lifted from me,
carried downstream
to become the future

will it know it is partly composed
from this moment's washing?

eventually, I will be eroded free from this form,
my grains ever smaller,
my essence loosed of boundary,
until I can say:

now I am the river.

LOVE ME, LOVE ME NOT

An orphaned child plucks rose petals,
counts hidden blessings:

they Love me,
they Love me not...
first I was left,
then I was bought

they Love me,
they Love me not...
sometimes I pay for sins
of my old family lot

they Love me,
they Love me not...
I am the stew gaining season
in the great boiling pot

they Love me,
they Love me not...
my road has lacked rest,
but my breast is made whole

shaped by the fields
flowering askew,
carved by the blades
of fate turned anew,
pledged by change
to become something more

covered in clay
by hands of the day,

rinsed to a shine
by purpose revealed,
over the yonder,
forward till healed

bronzed in the cauldron,
fired in the sun,
a fast talkin',
high steppin'
soul on the run

I could not have known
the depths of true Love,
without first tasting
loss and learning again
to stand by the fence
in the strongest wind
and not let go

and not let go.

WHEN I SHINE WHAT'S MINE

The runaway youth
turns over achingly,
a mountain of burden
avalanching cracked cares
deep into the mattress of night

then,
dawn breaks,
a golden yoke erupts
into the yielding black,
cobalt floods the morning,
an epiphany flies through
his mental window and gives him
fresh peace for the day

for a lifetime:

I cannot get that over there,
so I have to get this over here

I cannot taste the sweetest fruit
under my evading sun,
so I have to taste all the sweetness
in the bitter one

I can't hear the most beautiful song,
so I have to find beauty
in the song sung wrong

I can't shine what I don't have,
so I have to shine what's mine

I have to sing my own song,
paint my own portrait,
plant my own garden,
pick my own fruit,
unearth my root,
break my bread,
find my water

and then

find out that what's my own,
isn't mine alone

some soul somewhere,
and I, share

a song
a portrait
a garden
a fruit
root, bread, water

I am not alone,
my own is not mine alone...
I am a simple thread
in a crazy pattern,
a wild wick
in a blazing lantern

I am not alone,
I am the world,
and all of this
is rays of bliss

when I shine what's mine.

WILD HORSE

Daydreaming beneath the willow tree,
imagining himself as father horse
encouraging boy horse at his knee:

Young colt weary from weight
of early life's hazard,
sniffing scent of some peaceful beyond,
as long legs stretch and stride
from wobble to steady gait

nature's dawn brings thaw
to the crisp white grass
licking your hooves

softer passage awaits you along your path

filling your strong lungs
once more with chilled morning air,
you pause and reflect on your day of birth,
then gallop on with hints of full-grown
stallion in your manner,

always searching for your peaceful beyond

out there,
beyond somewhere.

WILD HORSE II

Far on the emerald meadow,
strolling through ropes of breeze,
the mentor asks the homeless youth:

why do you Love these horses so much?

the youth obliges with a smile:

a wild horse is a beautiful thing,
it will not ask human permission
to be or sing

such brazen steed doubts not its freedom,
all the world its rightful range,
boundless roaming does not come strange

a penned up horse is not the same,
its muscles surge at swing of stable gate,
but doubt befalls its forward gait

first steps tremble at the fate
of crossing beyond the binding fence
that is its comfort zone

a penned up horse
abdicates its majestic throne

I too have become like this,
afraid to gallop into my truth,
shrinking before the open gate

freedom is a dream, sown
into the imagination of those who own
their dreams and all they hold,
who set loose their fantasies
and dare live bright and bold

a wild horse is a beautiful thing,
it does not ask human permission
to be or sing

nor bare its nature,
nor rear and run

I dream of life like this,
free and racing with the sun.

FALLEN FRUIT

I am of my root, my root is of me,
we can never truly be divided,
we shall feed each other forever

I am because you were,
you are because I still am

I am beautiful
because I was born of beauty

I am flawed, and the child of flaw,
I have a lesson because of what I saw,

I have a song not kept by the law,
I am a winged thing, and will have my way,
I am sunlight, punctuating turbulent day

I am compassion, tendering on life's flaming grill,
I can open and trust you, if you dare and will

I am the fruit that fell from the tree,
that split open my bounty at the foot of a glory
only I may decipher

what you call my agony, I call my piper

I am led by what has befallen my fate,
soon I'll arrive at my potential's gate,
swing wide the doors, jump in the pool,

we'll all have a party, till some sensible fools
tell us it's time to hush all the noise

that's when I'll tell you the secret to girls,
the secret to boys

no... let me tell you now,
too many young need you to know this:

feed them what they *are*, and they'll become
what they *be:*

purposeful, powerful, possibility

life's newborn miracles grow in a field
only young spirits Love to visit

let us allow them their roots
when they go there to pluck them

they may return to us with hands full of bouquet,
and daydreams to last a lifetime.

FAMILIAR STEW

Me and my friends
used to play in mud puddles
whenever we could catch them

since the flood,
I don't think I'll play
in mud puddles anymore...
I don't have a sad song for you,
I just don't like remembering the mud,
the oozing water,
the things stuck inside

I like remembering the laughter we
passed around like bread,
the wild things we dared,
the shadows we fled

seeing traces of myself in other faces
makes me feel like
God took up some good clay,
made some masterpieces,
and kept the crumbs to the side
to make up *me*

I like feeling like I'm the leftovers
of some delicious meal,
so much better than feeling like
I'm the first and only of my kind,
something nobody's seen or tasted before

sometimes people swallow such food
just to be polite,
I want people to see me and salivate
because they've had something like me before
and they *Loved it*

I want to be the familiar stew,
the favorite cake,
the comfort food

I want to be the family recipe
passed down for generations,
not on yellowed paper
but from heart to heart

when the flood came,
I suddenly washed up on somebody's plate,
a strange and foreign food,
nobody recognized that I came from
a batch that still remains inside of me

I don't need to be stuffed with new recipes
to come out all right,
I need someone to taste *my* original recipe
and find that even through the flood
I am *still* a delicacy.

I SAY YES

Your Honor,
I am nine years old and not sure
what a forever family is, or a Loving home

I thought I had those things before

now you ask me whether standing here today
I can truly say I want to stay with this new
family I have come to know

if it means I don't have to stand up here
alone again in a court like this, I say yes

if it means I am no longer somebody's case,
I say yes

if it means no more home visits
that my friends ask me about, I say yes

if it means I get to keep all my stuff, I say yes

if it means I get to keep my language, I say yes

if it means I get to keep my school,
my teacher, my grade level, my friends, I say yes

if it means I get to stop being labeled, I say yes

if it means somebody will help me
remember my dear family, I say yes

if it means I can make mistakes
and not be returned like merchandise, I say yes

if I can keep my pet turtle, I say yes

if someone will tell me my high cheekbones are
beautiful, I say yes

if I get to go to family reunions and not be
whispered about, I say yes

if someone takes the time to understand
what life is like for me, I say yes

if I get to wake up and remember where I am,
I say yes

if I don't have to stop missing my first family,
I say yes

Forever and *Love* are words big people put on
posters to talk about children like me

me, I don't trust words on posters too much,
I trust the little things that make me feel big

I trust big things that don't make me feel little

I trust the truth even if it hurts,
'cause it can't hurt me more than a lie,
and I don't trust tomorrow, I trust today

so, Your Honor, if staying with my new family
means my heart learns peace starting today,

I Say Yes.

AMAZING GRACE

I am Spirit,
come to tell you my story

although I passed into here through Mother dear
and Daddy faded, my days soon thereafter were
cast in shadows ill paraded

monsters leapt from beneath my bed, stole away
my sleep... weary became my constancy

I, without a blanket to secure me from my
tremble, began the growing of my pain
the first days did assemble

then four new hands took me in,
woman tall and specked with graying hair,
man with cavern voice who sings *Amazing Grace*
softly in my ear

new-Mama always says to me:
Baby Son, you are my throne,
says she is regal, because she is graced with me

in these words I find comfort
like the fetal one I remember

when I flash back and shadows invite themselves
into my room where I seek peaceful sleep,
new-Daddy comes to me, soaks me in his arms
strums his vocal chords, vibration deep

Amazing Grace...
carries me to tranquility

I once was lost, but now am found,
was fearful, but now I sleep

universe is made not from stillness
but from movement,
is composed not of staleness, but of change,
I descend from that ocean,
was made to move from first wave
into this... circle of my begotten blessing

a part of me will always float in space,
the rest of me will always drown
in this Amazing Grace

I think I know what *kinship* means:
on this earth none are unrelated,
for related is the very *definition* of Life

relationship is the act of spirit
recognizing itself in another,
naturally loving our *self* inside the other

a joyful soul spends life finding itself in others,
what stupendous treasure hunt

relationship is fulfillment of destiny...
me, new-Mama, new-Daddy, we are not family
unusual, we are family *meant* to be

humanity's highest work is *to take care of,*
to take care of is to recognize essence,

honor and respect essence,
recognize other-essence in our own essence,
taking care of others *is* taking care of self

the beautiful ones who take care of me now,
I shall return unto them their glory tenfold,
by virtue of how I become the universe
and walk a peaceful soul

both young and elder are stationed
near the doorway between worlds...
when we tend to either we are
performing maintenance on the hinges that
ultimately swing for us, we lubricate the
passageway of our own birth and passing

we sing that *my home is over Jordan...*
yet young and elder occupy the shore
between mid-life and the river,
the river of *taking care of*, not condescendingly,
resentfully, false pride-fully, but humbly,
gracefully, thankfully, enduringly

our reward may not now be so evident,
but surely and truly if we lean forward,
we will hear whisper of our Amazing Grace

both the cared for and the caretaker
once were lost and now, in caring, are found

this is how our blindness may come to see

I grow weary, need to find my rest

please, won't you carry me?

OUR TEACHER IS THE DAY

A child begs for our surrender into Love:

Our teacher is the day

and in that day,
sage trees massage the sky,
for they discern that air
is their truest plumage
and not the leaf

our teacher is the day,
for life abundant courts us
with its lessons

you fear unbridling
your heart before me,
lest I pierce it for the offering,
yet your truest wound
comes from that very
surrender to fear

show me your heart
and all it holds,
for thereby may I know
you as human,
and in that knowing,
settle my unsettledness
about your purpose
on my path

for you in your humanness
are by default
the dust of my path,
the length of my striding,
the arc of my sojourn

the blood with which my feet
stain the road I traverse
is swelled with your corpuscle

my embrace of you
shall be evidence of... hope,
for my greatest test
on this shallow plain of earth
is that I see you,
not as the air encircling me,
but as my plumage,
and in strutting you,
I set *me* free

our teacher
is the day

the lessons blossom
endlessly.

CHILD SOLDIER

Sleep took over me in a tangle of vines
and a shower of rainy drops,
leaping down from umbrella of leaves
onto my dirt-streaked face

morning roused me with the same patter
of drops on my forehead, mouth, neck

in the gaining light I brushed my fingers
over my facial skin,
my fingers returned darkened red

I realized the raindrop patter of prior night
was now the bloody patter of the dead

my bullet-torn schoolmate lodged himself
in the trees above me during night

he knew he was dying as he nested there, like an
old elephant, he found his final resting place

he left me a final letter,
his blood a mournful goodbye across my face

in the mud of a far-off place,
I buried him in the weeping grove

my nineteenth goodbye since my family burned
in our straw home at dinner time

I was fifteen, my face lined
with a man's wrinkles, worry wrought

greed and seduction dug the trenches of our war,
bullets and bayonets dug the trenches where
my schoolmates now rest forever,
grief dug the trenches in my heart,
foreign governments dug my country's grave
with their *non-engagement*

memories dug the canals through which
my brothers and sister crawled back to me,
mostly at night, mostly when the palms
grew heavy with rain, sagged, and sighed

forest animal shrieks and howls sometimes
became merged with dreamt cries of my family
burning, while the nuts I had picked that day
lodged in my throat, pillowed in my mouth

by age eight my hands calloused
at the machete handle from clearing fields

at sixteen my calluses were killing pads
for an AK-47, my inseparable comrade
in the war that swept me up, held me tight

now I overdose on books about conquerors
on elephants in the Pyrenees,
to keep the stench of horror from my mind

now I am calloused of heart as people
from dainty lives give me their smiles and meals
and pride, seeking to stroke me into healing,
growing ever impatient with my emotional hide

now I lay me down to sleep, bound with five blankets,
lest my soul to creep, back to the groves where rain
changed in the night to blood,
and banished me from the season
where children find their normalcy

now I stow grain seeds beneath my nails,
anticipating days without food, despite the dainty
ones piling mountainous meals on the dining
table and smiling at me

back when I was seven,
before mother left for heaven,
she let me plant a garden beside her own

cabbage, squash, melons ripe,
carrots, yams, corn delight

each morning I dirtied my knees to tend and
weed, turn and water,
I saw how roots mingle in the earth and child
stalks survive beetles, sun, wind, even birth

I am sure the hate that singed our land,
turned our gardens black and left them sand

I wonder though if by some miracle
the roots remain, shocked and shaking in the soil

if such a thing is possible, hope may live
for the calming of my pain, and I may learn again,
to Love the patter of falling rain.

QUALIFIED

Dear Madam University President, I am writing you this letter to indicate my desire to be admitted to your school for the fall academic year. I submitted my application to the admissions office as required, but at age 17, and after 12 years in foster care and 7 foster care placements, I have learned that it is best to state my intentions to any and everyone who might have a stake in determining my future. I would like now to present to you my qualifications for admission as a student to your university:

I was taken from my mother at birth,
a rose plucked from earth,
I have spent 17 years developing
a capacity to overcome loss,
I laid baby brother in his grave,
said goodbye to 9 best friends...
I believe these meet your requirement
for what is called resiliency

I work well in relationships...
10 social workers have walked with me,
11 foster parents have fretted over me,
5 ministers, 4 pastors, 3 priests, 2 deacons,
a medicine woman, *and* a fortune teller
have prayed over me

if you need a student leader, I'm the one...
desperation to survive gave me a voice

and the will to use it,
I am resourceful and will seek out
campus resources I require,
just as I have had to do to make
my way through the child welfare system

and how would I get along with my
dormitory roommates?
I have already had 27 roommates,
if you count my foster siblings

I possess strong writing skills...
I have written long poems of prayer and desire
across my own heart in the black nights
that chased away my sleep

I deal well with turning negative into positive...
caring adults too numerous to count
have condescended to me,
from this I learned the grace such that
should my professors condescend to me
with low expectations,
I shall return to them only my dignity

I know you are looking for team players,
good campus citizens...
I understand how important it is
for people to feel secure in their relationships,
this has been the desert I have crossed
from family to family, friend to friend,
I will make every student I come across
feel valued, valid, and full of voice

I have no choice,
these are the things I need,

to deny them to others would be hypocrisy,
this is what foster care has made me see

blood ran red from rivers of self-mutilation,
I carved into my flesh the story of my strife,
but from this I learned the recipe for healing,
now my rivers run as passion for music and
history, both take me beyond my pain
on a journey of jazz, soul, and human reciprocity

I am not afraid to ask questions in the classroom,
questions were my only protection from the
flawed intentions of my care providers,
of my authorities

I am good at problem solving, trouble shooting,
and strategizing, after all, I created *my own* case
plan, so planning my coursework is no great task

enduring all night study sessions are child's play
to me, I have spent a thousand nights
studying my escape from life's limbo

I am a kite in flight... social pressure, what you
call *conformity*, is but a flimsy string to me
that I snap as I soar to my destiny

forgiveness? easy... my daily meditation is
forgiveness for those who abandoned me,
made fun of me, judged me, scorned me,
labeled me gave up on me, ran scared from me

and trust? who better than a foster child to have
the courage to trust, when so many times people
have done nothing but cause hurt and pain?

I withstood that bitter rain
learned to keep the water,
let the salt run down the drain

compassion is a shelter I found from the storms of
my troubles, helping others on campus would be a
reflex to me, a mentor lives inside me,
this I already see

charity is often thought to be the *giving* of a gift,
but too often I have been the *object* of that charity,
so I know the truth: to be charitable is to honor
the beauty of another soul , thereby opening
yourself up to that beauty, *receiving* its hidden
gift... when we help another, we are not *giving*
charity, we are *receiving* it,
from life's great beauty waiting within

I'm an A-plus student of sincerity,
people have always felt the need to be dishonest
with me, they say oh, we only want the best for
you, and, your roots aren't worth talking about,
and, if only you would bond or attach to us,
your problems will be solved, your trouble
flushed... I knew better, I *crushed* dishonesty,
on the path to intimacy with my own reality

I was a child of pain as much as of joy,
both were my story that I will tell the world

I will educate myself,
craft my own Declaration of Independence,
a Song of Interdependence,
of the importance of relationship,
my declaration will be a cry for truth,

a drumbeat for honesty, a distaste for prejudice

as a teacher of what it means to overcome,
I will claim my nobility... I'm cold corrected,
make crazy beats from the basement of my
destiny, and the rest of me, yeah it's dusted and
rusted, but it sure isn't busted,
I just need a chance to find romance in the way I
learn to Love this world that's tripped me up

triumph over trouble is my cup,
and my cup runneth over the rubble,
I can make rose gardens rise from toxic grounds,
I *must* have skills...
I am not a tarnished adjective,
I am a positive noun,
I can't slow down, I'm almost there, where?
to Peace and Possibility,
to becoming the whole of me

I've attended 14 schools,
learned 198 foster family rules,
had to catch up on spools and spools
of foster family stories and allegories,
rituals and routines

had to tolerate a whole rack of family tastes in
food, music, threads,
not to mention make all those beds,
had to swallow my own song 158,716 times,
been reprimanded for committing the crimes
of not learning my foster families' songs fast
enough, not opening up and trusting quick
enough, not forgetting the past enough, not
conquering my pain enough, not smiling enough

not being grateful enough, not talking enough,
not forgiving enough, for all sorta stuff, but
mainly for being too rough... around the edges,
so everything I touched tended to bleed,
that's my main crime, I do concede

I had to polish up myself, learn to get along, go
along, wait a long... time before my own needs are
quenched, this is evidence of capacity to endure,
to cope, to not require immediate gratification,
all reasons I can succeed at your university

in fact, I believe once I start college I'll major in
biology, chemistry, psychology, sociology,
history, physics, economics, communications,
English, foreign language, creative arts,
and most of all politics,
because I've already developed the skills those
majors require, *just* to get through my childhood

my *life* is my résumé,
sure as sunlight seeks the day

Madam University President, if I may share with
you a summary of what I have learned from my
time in the system about the nature of human
relations, *that lesson is this:*

the child in need is not the mouth we feed,
the wound that bleeds, the soul that grieves,
the falling leaves

no, a child in need is the fertile seed, the sacred
creed, the unpolished bead, the opposite of greed,
the lie now freed to sprout from seed

when we teach, mentor, raise, guide this child,
it is *WE* who are blessed, *OUR* soul caressed,
our stress less messed, *our* restlessness made less,
our own pain finessed, *our* cold places warmed in
the breast of chest, *our* tenderness less suppressed,
our callousness regressed, *our* prejudice confessed
and given rest, *our* fears past crest,
our special-ness dressed and pressed,
our Truth made spark, then flame, then zest,
and from that passion springs the rest:
our fullest shining humanness

So, Madam University President, I am writing
you this letter to introduce you to a child of the
system, and I humbly submit to you that *precisely
because of* my life journey, I am *exponentially*
qualified. This is my story. I hope you have
enjoyed the ride.

HOME AT LAST

I journey
bold and bright

make my bed by
folding up the night

I sit on moon,
ponder stars

play my dreams
like lofty music bars

kiss waking sun
who smiles and
walks with me

a flower shy and bright
blossoms on the path

it wears my blushing face

I am found
and home at last.

I AM THE PARADE

Beneath the bridge, in the rain,
still far from the warmth of dawn,
the mountainous voice rises from earth:

Your soul pours out now, you've suffered so long,
all you needed was to stop your madness of
motion and sit beside the grass

see how I have made it a shocking green for you?

see how I have tinted the light, as in a dream?

this waking life is the true dream,
a fantasy, if you let it be

let go the chaos of lost souls,
don't join that parade,
I made you for the ecstasy of dissolving in long
baths of solitude, that your soul may awaken to
its belonging with all things

you must walk through the blistering waterfall of
loneliness, absolute chilling aloneness, before you
reach the other side where I make days a dream

the souls circling you chattering, are your angels
at work deciding how to entice you to hear true
music and leave alone the noise of human wailing

bear for a moment this pain of separation

once you tear your *Self* from flesh, you will open
up into your final fantasy, realizing only then that
you have always been in the company of
Creation... you could not be less alone

you are the center of the largest party,
here there is no other, for all exists within you,
all around you comes from your own breath

taste the mint leaf,
you were the one who gave it sweetness,
the smell of jasmine is from your own scent

stop wasting your whole life seeking others,
racing behind the parade like a panicked child,
afraid no one will notice you

you are the parade,
it is your panic that goes unnoticed,
parades stop not for the forlorn

you are not left in the desert,
you are the desert's leavings

sip my hidden water and rise up,
from this taunting earth.

HOLLOW REED IN THE HANDS OF LOVE

Barefoot in the sand of dunes,
bathed in the blushing sky of dawn,
dressed in white linens flapping gently,
a young man and woman face each other,
to be wed

the groom, on the verge of this, the first true
family of his whole life, shakes before the one to
be his wife... makes his vows:

I am a hollow reed in the hands of Love

she shall play me as she chooses

my grain polished in her natural oil

her wind a rustling wave through my instrument

I was shaped long ago,
refined through strategic seasons

her lips were always ready
for this moment of my arrival

little could I have known that in the summer heat
and the cicada choir, she would be my survival

moon sets fat, morning balloons to brightness

this day is come into my breast and perched

I am the wild one, braying at the sky

I am the settler on the dusty trail
who never questions why

I am the recalcitrant longing, now letting go

I am the crying rain, I am the melted snow

I bent down to pick up a precious stone
and picked up God's Intent

my heart shuddered, now I feel Me dent

my tin pan stands no chance,
my chalice is set to weep,
my steel drum is welted,
my furnace no longer sleeps

Love is blowing her mint breath
through my waiting reed

music leaves from my every opening,
I, astounded at the deep

I never knew such a hollow place as I
could be filled like this,
so blown open,
so flooded, Godly,
and of Grace.

WHERE GOOD THINGS GO

The eight-year-old stands before her class
draped in a flowered dress, beaming with
revelation almost unseen in such youth

she has no notes, no props

she begins:

my grandmother is in the trees,
so I go to the trees, smell their bark,
scent of her perfume escapes the wood

child pauses a moment to gauge their reaction:
silence
...so she continues

my favorite doggy is in the grass,
I go and sit on the soft blades,
there I can pet him and stroke him

my Aunt Chalice, she is in the water,
I go down by the creek and play with her,
she always tickles my feet

my babysitter is in the fruit trees in our backyard,
I pick a peach or pear every day, slowly eat it,
babysitter always kisses me,
makes me feel good inside

my baby brother, he is in the garden,

I go and sleep there when the sun is out

he tells me secrets
from inside the blossoms of the flowers,
from the bosom of tomatoes,
from the foot of cornstalks

he lets me know when rain is
coming or when the soil is lonely

more silence...
then the teacher asks:
how are these people where you say they are?

and the eight-year-old, finishing her turn
at show-and-tell, answers with surprise:

where else do you think they would go
when they leave us?
they pass into the places we Love
so they can be with us forever

returning to her seat,
she thinks to herself contentedly
and with a smile:
where have these people been all their lives?

EVAPORATING

At the end of the school year,
the young man sits and shares
with his favorite teacher what he has learned
about having someone believe in you:

I allow my mind to describe a rock, and am left
more able to imagine the grain it bears,
also, the mountain whose earth it shares

the object is not life's nectar, the gathering of it is

the place is not the point,
how we occupy that place is

the way is not so glorious, our walking of it is

you sang me your song and thought I was your
audience, instead, I was the notes your lips
ushered

your breath was my coat, its moisture my skin I
shed as I left you and became cloud

it was like stepping from a warm
bath and evaporating

what I became was not so important
as the fact that I did...

change.

MOSES IN YOUR MIDST

Story time, and the 15-year-old mentor
shares with her pensive young friend
a tale of how she sees both their lives:

So, the story goes..
small, tender-hearted baby
born to his mother dear in the desert, by the river

taken from the womb
to the post-natal room,
then foster care, then adopted into a home
with the expectation that he not let his Truth
shine out

that he not speak about it, think about it,
feel about it, be about it

and though he was well Loved,
the pain, it came... never ending flood
in sheets of rain
no relief, just private tears and pillow stains

and he asked, the small child, he asked:
God, why hast thou forsaken me?
why am I alone?

and God answered:
Child of Mine,
I have not forsaken you,
I have given you life

I have torn your world asunder,
this is My Divine plan,
not a simple blunder

you must be cast in this fire,
for I need you to be a certain stone

only this fire can bring the right shine
to the Light in you I need

you must have patience...
though the nights are long,
you must endure, like My child Job,
you must endure

you must have faith, though the Light has yet to
dawn before you, you must believe with the depth
of My child Abraham,
you must believe

you will see, My child,
you are not alone, for I am with you
in the streets, and in the home

the pain you feel is My path laid down for you,
walk it to Me,
you are the salt,
I am The Sea

and the day came
when the child became a man
and found his voice, and in speaking,
a woman who heard his voice came to him

she was Black as fertile earth
and weary from wear, her eyes watery,
her body shaken by the touch of Light

and it was God
who spoke through her and said:
Child, you are *Moses*...
taken from your people at birth
so that you may live
among those who strain to see the whole of you,
so you may see the truth in their hearts,
know the true breadth of humanness

this circumstance has given you sight
unlike others into the truth of
your own heart and that of your people

you have come to know the Divine
meaning of your people's pain,
for their pain has been returned to you
a hundredfold

you have swallowed this ocean of tears,
kept it close by your heart,
that you may not stray from My plan for you

you must go forth
and speak of what you have known,
you must tell your people
that God has spoken these words

and God spoke such:

Behold... a certain number of souls,
children born into the abyss

where children are not meant to be

you must not feel sorry for these children,
rather, feel responsible for these children,
for within them lies a truth restless for daylight

I have borne them a pain
that has given them a vision,
and among them are ones who will
rise up among their people
and serve as teachers,
messengers,
leaders

take notice of these children
for beyond the stories
of abuse, neglect, poverty, violence, disease,
they are Moses in your midst

where despair is in the life of a child,
you must bring that child home,
for there is Moses in your midst

take care with these tender souls,
for these children shall go forth
as a people with passion in their hearts
and a great vision,
for I have spoken early into their ears:
You shall be unto Me a holy nation

where a child is left un-kept,
you shall keep her,
where a soul is left in tatters,
you shall bring repair

mourn not your loss of comforts
as you comfort lives in need,
for your needs shall be satisfied
by My Divine breath, which shall fill you up
and make you whole, exceedingly

you shall be that cloud above, unencumbered,
for you will have fulfilled My word

and where they bid you
do your works for private gain,
respond with a soulful heart
and actions for public good,
make your neighborhoods a temple
unto your kin

feed into your homes
lessons of your people's legacy,
stories of miracle and wonder,
let no child be unexposed
to the possibility of triumph over pain

let no child dance alone,
as I have made their joy
a thing to be witnessed,
their celebrations a cause
for you to pause your frantic pace

let no dream from children
fade in the morning
to be not captured in the net of day,
for child dreams are My bounty from the sea,
harvest them well,
do not assume that I will
always make the sea so plentiful

even when these children pull from you in fear,
extend yourselves to them,
make of your arms a bridge they may cross...
they seek a way over troubled water,
play well your part

let no child song be solo in its singing,
join them in that breath of joy,
let them know their melody is a good one,
they have music to offer the world

if they believe they are needed,
they will rise up like morning glories and stroke
the sky with beauty you have never known

keep no dust upon their shoulders
from inattention,
make them feel your eyes in constant upon
their backs, that they are known,
they are seen, they are cradled in your Love and
care and respect, for all the days

they will test your resolve, these children,
as I have tested theirs,
for faith is made of painful things

but watch for their produce,
for I shall give unto them
manna bread that only they may harvest
and bring into your homes...
one day it is they who will
fill your plates and sustain your soul

shepherd them all the way of their path,

for they lead you into the place where
the sea is parted on the left and on the right,
and through which you must pass
if ever your kind will find freedom

if ever the screams of slaves
shall be pulled wet from the sea
and made into Freedom's exclamation

if ever the warriors cut down
as they stood for your dignity
are to testify in that Higher court
on the day of your long last justice

if ever the rose thorns that
have insulted your skin
all these generations
are to bear blossom
and bathe you in the fragrance
of children faring well

if ever you are to
find faith in that I am
the wood
and I am the stone
that is your home

and that *I am that I am,*
that these children *are* that I am,
therefore as you reclaim for them
their sense of safety and security,
you recapture your own chance of salvation

for a new season has come...
these are days of endless nights,

and your sleeping time
should cause you shudder

too many injured adult souls
seep discernment from their vessels

such seepage floods good homes
into the waters of jeopardy,
such that the tide flows through bedrooms
and lifts children from where they lay...

and out the door
into the vastness of systems made
not from the substance of your people's legacy,
but from hearts and minds
in blind lurch and stumble

know that
when those who would oppress your people
build vessels whose charge is to carry your
own children to salvation, the only consequence
is that these vessels will come
to hold your children in life's limbo

and neither transport them to a better
shore nor return them back to
the first shore restored

when those who would oppress
your people build vessels
to carry your children,
beware that *I* have not built
those vessels

they are crafted of the impulse

of imperfect men,
and what you inherit from
that manner of lumber
is not My word
nor My way

but the word and way
of a spirit who would
lash that lumber so
leakage may steal aboard
and drown your precious offspring

I have given you
My word
and My way
since long ago,
before this land you call free,

you have always
cared for your children
according to My Heavenly inspiration

It was I who whispered
creativity into your ears,
upon which you found ways
even in your struggles
to make good hearted people
a part of your family
even without the bond of blood

kinship is your word for this

I call it My Divine order,
for you shall Love your neighbor
as yourself,

and family is a richness you cannot inflate

It was I who tapped
truth into your hearts,
that you would speak stories
to your young ones of values
and lessons they must gain
to grow to productive lives
in a world where foe and friend
speak with same tongue,
a world where their origins might
be cause for their destruction,
a place where their ways
might be seen as less than human,
their spirituality spat away in fear

who knows better
the substance your children
will require than you who have
survived upon that same stalk
in your own endless storm?

where you go in seek of answers
for brokenhearted children,
go first unto yourselves,
for there is where the hearts
were broken first

go not to those
who would dictate to you
a recipe for their own taste

where you would build a home,
make it for a child,
where you would grow a family,

make it for a child,
where you create community,
make it for a child,
where you construct a temple,
make it for a child

for where I am worshipped
must you make a home
for My children

do yourselves this favor,
because with these children,
there is Moses in your midst

for every child who cries,
let there be a family
who would teach the ways of Love
and self Love,
how to conquer prejudice,
and give one's life for one's people

let your lessons flow
from your every mouth
and drip from your cloth
to puddle around your every step

for, the moment you
leave that footprint behind,
a child takes to hands and knees
and drinks from that water hole

beware,
there... drinks Moses in your midst

let there be for every shelter,

one child dream to protect,
one dawn for every darkness,
one feast for every hunger,
one family for every solitude,
one community for every family,
one people striving for one truth,
one Love for one purpose,
one faith in the value of every life,
one hope for one fear,
one joy for one tear,
one peace for one war,
one home for one life run wild,
one temple for one blessed child

each one,
Moses in your midst...
give them shelter,
they will give you
manna from My Heaven,
freedom from My fist

careful with them

careful

they are
Moses in your midst.

FALLEN LEAVES

Youth illuminates guardian
during their weekly walk through woods:

When autumn leaves fall from trees
they beautify ground,
fertilize earth,
become substance for new birth

when we children fall from families,
we too can beautify the ground,
we just need someone to
hold us sacred for who we are

your tears of sympathy
rot our leafiness

your celebration
breaks us beautifully down to earth

in that sacred soil
we fallen child leaves
cup ourselves
to carry extraordinary

we mimic the triumph
of sprouts who breach
soil's crust,
we become fertile
and all the while
gorge on youthful wanderlust.

CREEPING VINES

Stage left,
a quiet brook

stage right,
a nightingale on the look

down stage,
the sweetly melancholic youth
begins his soliloquy
in the final gloaming
beneath a satiated orb of moon:

Culture...
does anybody know your essence?
you claw like creeping vines
through blood and bones,
saturate the walls
where humans dwell,
cast elusive spell
like petroglyphic
Love sonnets
written in child's
white chalk script
in black of
deepest cave

Culture,
you make us crave
Love:
I Love it when you talk like that
Love:

I Love it when you stroke my back
Love:
I Love it when you take my child heart
in your hands and caress
the topography of my... Love

you don't try to shape
my heart in your hands
like so much passive clay,
squeezing gray dying through
the breaches between your fingers,
you know that would
rupture creeping vines within
this pumping, glistening,
condensation of a stream
that holds direct VIP status
with Creation

and therefore goes my... culture...
does anybody know your breath
as it takes its scent within my mouth?
and who around here knows
your tendency to curl in warm currents
through my mind

making thoughts dance
like jitterbugging, jukebox playing,
gin swigging
common folk
in the sweat box
of a crammed joint by the
mosquito clouded river
on a full moon August night?

oh my flutter taking flight

making my thoughts
dance like fresh oil
on the water coated griddle,
like rain drops popping
off taut tense trampoline
of a hairdo done
with too much pomade?

like sweetness
doing calisthenics
in my lemonade?

dance like,
I child see world with eyes
naïve and wild,
make whole picture fresh
like mama's bestest apple pies,
make old ways
bring silly questions to my mind

like if you say you Love me,
why do you run from
my creeping vines?

is Love therefore
the condensation
of the chemistry
between affection
and discomfort,
browned in the oven
of intellectual confusion,
blackened over the
broil of emotional fear?

and should this be that

meal that carries me,
lifts me,
makes my soul
swell from deflated balloon
to brazen plump and mighty
planet that in adult form
seeks to orbit according to
the essence of my culture?

do I drift?
let me say it like this:
when I touch my lips,
that minute act has roots

when I cry at purple sky,
emotion comes from a place
that *lives*...
maybe not in your time,
or your place,
or your people, heart, home, dreams

my emotion
comes from a place that lives
and seeds with a million
billowing strokes
of fertility
the soil, rain, sunlight
that give the Divine right
for my creeping vines
to vein my heart,
stain my eyes,
wane the storm
of my discontent

for my culture

smells like this, tastes like this
feels like this, grows like this

and comes from,
comes from,
molecule, ionic particle,
atomic dance, spirit romance
across the ages,
turning pages
of generation
to leave I child
in your hands,
not as clay
but as a truth
that comes from
a place that lives

pray I every moment
of every night
that as I child
am in your hands,
you put away your
crushing grasp

and Love my,
I mean bleed and Love my,
I mean humble and Love my,
I mean thank Divine Sky
and Love my
creeping
vines...

OUTSIDE YOUR WINDOW

What were you imagining
when you brought me to the place
that for you is home?

you could not have been thinking
of me,
I am the last thing this place is

I am a copper storm of tears
beating against your cold window

the slew of my pieces
falls down wailing against
the glass

I am beating
both to get in and to catch
your attention

the woods of this non-seeing
are swallowing me

your closed conception of me
opens a door for the wolves to enter

your fear is a pallid finger
stirring a vortex into existence,
your avoidance, a sharp breath
gusting me to cusp of flush

you know the next step don't you?

many things drown in the ocean,
often unnoticed or misdiagnosed

most of us are too busy to notice
the nature of a drowning,
we aren't looking directly at
the soon to be departed

her thrashing escapes our periphery,
this is how we would have it,
for to truly notice a drowning, and do nothing,
is a tortuous death itself for the nothing-doer

I am the night's bleating rain
against your cold window

I make patterns like ant columns
in the sand on your hard glass
as I fall

I do not fall intentionally,
this is not manipulation,
that would require my belief
that you would catch me

I am headed down the glass
to the graveyard of souls deposed

and what were you imagining?
my compassion ends this poem:

perhaps we both can recover
if we leave our souls on the fire
to become something new.

CAN I CALL YOU MOM AND DAD?

Can I call you Mom?
not just when the sun is shining melancholy
and the house is full of laughter honey sweet,
but also when my fear becomes a monster
from which I cannot retreat...
can I call you Mom?

when the wind whistles to me that I
am something cast away, and I respond
with sullenness or simply surrender to
the breaking waves upon sifting shores within
my breast... can I call you Mom?

I know you're there for me
when I get good grades
and take out the weekly trash,
but when I find messy ways to lick my wounds
from being discarded like that trash...
can I call you Mom?

will you wait for my bluer sky?
for my waterfall to come?
I fear you will give up on me like others did,
like others do,
that's why I'm steady testing you

I need to see the boundary of your faith in me,
my soul searches endlessly
for the proof that I am truly Loved,
not just parts of me but the whole of me,
all of me needs to find a meadow where

I can finally rest peacefully...
can I call you Dad?

will you do more than play catch with me?
will you cradle me in your gentle sea?
rock me gracefully into my sleep at night?
or will your heart give up on me
when we fight or see this world in different light?

does my pain have a passport to live here too?
or will you deny my hurt at the door,
making me drop my tears silently? privately?

if so I fear I will drown having never swum
in your gentle sea,
so if I'm rude or wrong or just plain bad...
can I call you Dad?

when other children scorn the skin of me,
will you actually be there for me?
will you bleed with me?

I know people look at me and see
a tornado spinning recklessly,
will you look and see the truth of me?
will you? will you see the all of me?
or am I only in your eyes to be
the imitation of your *own* beauty?

I've been bouncing through this world
like a basketball, but no one wants to
take a shot with me,
no one believes I can find the hoop,
that I can score,
but if you just send me on my proper arc,
I know I can win the game...

can I call you Mom and Dad?

or does fostering the whole of me
make your soul run sad?
will you let me take my story out from
under the bed and share it in the living room?
or will our family sweep away my truth with
avoidance broom?

can I bring my passions with us to the park?
you like the rising sun,
I like star gazing in the dark

can I pull my fears from the sock drawer
and show them to you?
or will you consume yourself with convincing me
that I have nothing to fear in your loving home?

my fears are real, but if you won't allow
me them honestly,
that would be my monstrosity,
see I need to know if you are down with me,
down in the trench where I walk through life

that way, with your company, I'll have the
strength to cut through my strife,
leave the trench,
I'll find my solid ground, learn to shine my light

can you, will you, foster me?
will you let me foster you?
I can show you new things too,
like how to Love an imperfect soul
in a way you never thought you'd do,
and if ever it were meant for you and I to part,

I pray that you would rest peacefully
knowing that for a priceless season
you gave this child, me, a reason to believe
he could make it in this world

because when I talked, you truly listened,
when I shined, it was your heart that glistened

when I ached inside, you never lied
about your heart's frustration,
you let my trauma breathe,
become my own salvation

because you let me sing my song
even if you didn't know that tune,
you let me Love October
just like you Love June

because you found the courage to face your
prejudice about that part of me
that discomforted you,
because you did not treat me as charity
but as your Golden Opportunity

because you realized that you did not just
foster me, but that I also fostered you,
because in your hands, your humble hands,
I found that meadow where I discovered
that I am beautiful and that I belong

because you fought the bitter social wind
and swam upstream on my behalf

because of all of this, you will have given me
my sweetest kiss, my forever bliss,
my rainbow painted in words like this:

this child, this soul, withstood the rain
overcame the pain, caught the Glory Train
shall never return, to despair again

if this is what we are to be as family,
I will walk this earth and make you proud,
your imperfect beauty will always shine
forth from me

can I call you Mom?
can I call you Dad?
I can?
Good,
you can't see it,
but inside, my heart is glad

I Love you Mom,
I Love you Dad.

MY FIRST KISS

Morning Mommy,
Morning Daddy

I had a dream last night,
it was a good dream,
felt like cotton candy on my tongue,
felt like my skin warm under morning sun

I was a big girl in the dream,
I was a mommy too...
I was sitting in my white nightgown
during indigo night
under crescent moon

I was writing you both a letter,
it went like this:

Mommy, Daddy, I remember my first kiss...
the one you both gave me that first
night in your home when you tucked me in

you both kissed me on my lips, at the same time,
it was then I knew that you were mine...

my first kiss it felt like this:

like I was a rose and all my thorns just
dropped to the ground, it was a song,
an amazing sound, it felt like grace,
amazing grace, had come to me

it felt like my tears were now the sea,
felt like floating on the ocean wide,
felt like crossing over to the other side

the side where children don't have to
run and hide, the side where bacon scent
fills the house at sunrise, and I'm not scared
no more to wipe the sleep from my eyes

'cause I know this day will greet me good
with sweet tea and harmony between my
family and me

it felt like a promise of something glowing,
like rust washed from around my heart,
felt like my panic slowing

felt like rain that knew my dry spots,
like wind, sweet breeze that carried me
like ground for once beneath my feet

like rainbows dancing,
the sky a brilliant blanket sheet...
my first kiss, it felt like this

the next morning my life with you began,
I remember things you thought I didn't know,
I remember how you feared I wouldn't grow
to Love you like you Loved me so

feared my heart would freeze from past pain
and I would grow silent like winter snow,
I heard your whispers through bedroom door,
how you worried one day I would be
yours no more

but by then my heart had grown a place inside
for you, a garden for which your flowers
alone would do...
I was a child but even I knew:
my roots had taken hold in you

even if one day I would
have to leave your space,
my heart's garden would always
be our family reunion place

I grew this in my heart for you,
because when I cried,
you kept my tears and used them
for a swimming pool
where we swam as
family in the substance of *my* life

you dared to get wet in what I was,
dared to swallow my salt along with yours,
showed me my water *is* clean enough for you

you kept my tears and filled a place
in your home with them,
this was to be my reflection pond,
a place at home where I could go and
see the image of myself

sometimes I looked ugly like a porcupine,
some days I looked pretty and called myself
Clementine, but every day I lived with you,
you preserved my reflection pond so I could
see myself and know I was more than rumor,
I was true

not only that... you drank from my pond
so I could see myself in you...
you said so many times: *we Love you...*
but I've heard such words before,
then the truth was shown,
that I was to be the cast out stone

it was only when you said the words,
then swallowed me,
that I truly believed I was
an orchid floating in your sea

Ma and Pa, I remember my first kiss,
the satin of your skin,
pillows of your lips,
coffee on your breath,
Pa's hands on Mommy's hips

I remember that first kiss,
doorway to my future bliss,
now I am a mommy too,
and I want to tell you what I've learned:

foster is a funny word,
child comes to us a hummingbird,
fluttering nervous tiny thing,
frantic beating of her wings,
hungry starving daring thing,
darting dancing wishing she could sing
like other birds and have her song listened to
enjoyed... understood

child comes to us a hummingbird,
flighty prancing hoping thing,
praying this family will let her sing,

searching for that safe place to land,
finally able to rest her wings,
those fragile resilient soulful wings

a child comes to us a hummingbird,
a jazzy soulful freestyle groove,
seeking our family nectar,
dreaming of its sweetness inside her
private heart

she has come to us with *her* song,
seeking *our* sweetness,
this is reciprocity...
we her family learn her song,
sing it back to her all life long

she fills her vessel with harvest of a blessed home,
moves forward with her wealthy life,
she flies, full of us and fresh of wing,
but she *must* fly, she is hummingbird,
she has songs to sing

our Love has become her,
our Love has *become* her,
she sings new word,
she is blessed grounded hummingbird

With that, the six-year-old kissed her mommy
and daddy on the lips and ran off to wash up for
breakfast. She smelled bacon in the house.

Her dream was good.

FOLLOW ME

Her heart journal entry:

I too have been to the mountaintop...
you would not believe
the future I have seen

I have found the human heart

it grows in the Cave of Longing,
just beyond the Woods of Belonging

you have to follow the River of Solitude
to find it beating in a Pool of Love

the cave is hidden
in a giant Moss of Fear

I know Solitude,
therefore I can find my way
through Belonging

I can recognize Longing
when we get there

when we do we'll have to
trample down the Moss of Fear

I've done this before...
I'll be your guide
to the human heart

Follow me.

SCRAPS

More of her heart journal entries:

Everybody looks at me,
nobody sees me.

Who writes the law
that says anyone who wants me
can have me?

I want a law
that says anyone who has me
has to want me

ALL OF ME.

They don't know this yet,
one day I'll shine,
they'll stop and feel,
I am the eternal sunrise,
I am,
I be,
I will.

People want to solve my problems,
people are my problems,
they need to solve themselves.

I am a pebble
bouncing between boulders
who believe they are stroking
me with feathers...
their touch feels like stone.

I exist
behind the blinding mist
your prejudice
casts upon my bliss,
look deeper and discover,
I exist.

ice cream, dreams, promises:
things that melt away...
I want to live in the place
where melted things stay.

I hear whispers
from far and aching shores,
it is my great and distant Amma,
she whispers to light a fire
and to keep me warm

even on sunny days
my heart is soaked with whispers.

MY NAME IS "BEAUTIFUL"

On the upper left corner of the bunk bed,
the corner up against the wall,
she carved a series of musical notes
into the bed post with a spoon she took
from the kitchen and hid during the day
in the pouch of her stuffed animal kangaroo

each night she carved a single note
long after her new family had passed into sleep,
the notes were flats and sharps and ran crooked
down the post from left to right

each note represented the substance of
that particular day as it melted into her,
a mist snaking into the pores of her skin,
becoming her

over a period of three years she kept
inscribing her daily passages like weather
reports on the soft fading wood,
the post became a tattooed trunk
littered with a symphony

her new father noticed her etchings,
so did her new mother,
new brother cousin sister best friend,
none knew their meaning

though each tried to ask,
her answers were always the same:

these notes are my music,
the music is my name,
the music is my name

she told herself this
almost as a chant she bathed herself in,
especially when pain battered against her heart,
a monsoon of side-swept tears tearing
at the lake of emotion deep within

the music is my name

only she knew the meaning of this music,
knew the beautiful truth of her name...
it would remain a secret she kept tucked
like a Love letter inside the folds
of her child heart

one day at the breakfast table
she announced to her new family:

these many days I have spent in this family
have been some of the richest of my life,
you have been so good to me,
yet I know I remain in your heart
and in the eyes of this community
cause for worry, rumor, stigma,
carrier of a story that sheaths my truth

so now I want to introduce
you to my true name,
that which I call myself
in music on my bedpost,
and in the auditorium
of my private thoughts

silence around the table

I call myself this name to counter
the well-intended silhouette that follows me,
the ideas in people's minds that bend
their perception of my light into illusion

because you have been so kind to me,
let me introduce you to my music,
which is my truest name

she debuts her deepest soul and sings:

my blossom yawns,
its morning dawns,
unfolding of my flower
has seized the hour,
what glory comes
a'splashing through
the light of this
newborn day...

her family, stunned

she concludes:
the music is my name and...

my name is *Beautiful.*

DECLARATION OF THE ADOPTIVE CHILD

We who walk the road of whispers do render this declaration of the adoptive child:

When grown bodies fail to nurture those draped in tenderness whose growing is incomplete and what's more has been disrupted by way of rupture, displacement, separation, dislocation, and transplantation, we so assaulted must act.

We hold in this place of conjure that men and women who have shed the unique skin of that most peculiar childhood should take hold the reins of self-definition in word, idea, and action, and set the course for freedom that their kin in circumstance would follow:

Freedom from abeyance by the fears of men; freedom from vulnerabilities of the latent voice of youthful in-articulation; freedom from quiescence before the agendas of those who have not walked that certain path; freedom from the withering erosion to esteem and identity come from stigma, prejudice, and devaluation on the basis of our life's occasion.

Freedom yet to tell a story and stand by the truth of it, no matter the offense to the sensitivities of the powerful or the moneyed; freedom from the blight of unjust tradition, dehumanizing conformity, and misguided missives.

Above all that we should set the course for freedom to live among the world of children as divinely worthy of but the best that adult-kind can hew from the mountainous disarray that is a child's life gone astray. For we are not special in the way that a comet is special amongst stars but special still in that the light of individual distinction and purpose shines within us, as with all children.

Our face is revealed on the slate hillside emergent beneath the receding glacier of myth. Our countenance is set in defiance against cast down eyes, for let it be known here and to the cusp of imagination's sweet limit that we are not charity, no pitiable soul-less mass. Who would adopt us has in fact presently been adopted *by us*. Our partnership is no less than equal. No more tarnished by the condescension of favor than is birth itself.

Look to the clamor on the horizon that is this global society's future. Our merriment if it strikes a wicked note upon the ear's drum is simply the sound of freedom at long last come. We know that look in the eyes of the adoptive one who has laid to rest her long nights of query toward life's providence. We know the daunting length of the circle traversed from birth to rupture to replant to reunion. We are intimate with the meaning of union, that lifelong consequence of choice: choice to shed away, rise, embrace, *become*.

We cast new light on biological strands in the quilt human and give hope to intimacies of the spirit. We are evidence of the fragility of bonds and contentment, even as we are whisper of resilience. Desolate is not the substance of our heart. The precise health of peace is our comportment to no lesser degree than for any other child or child of childhood, for childhood's season too spawns its own offspring in the form of adult complexities.

This is a tale of gleaming opportunity and fertile ambivalence. The broken chains of our familial fabric rust themselves from neglect yet become our amulet of personality, like coral colonies grown bright and bountiful on the backs of broken leftovers in the sea. Our hearts take hold and surge forth brazen in the tide of our reconstituted sense of family.

Friction has shaped and fitted us with an eyepiece whose lens takes us deep into the heart of a child's pristine flower of insecurity. From this vantage it strikes us that we are the ultimate authority beneath only Divine Wisdom in that moment when souls strive to erect a home in theory, legislation, policy, action, and in a child's heart: A home tangible and intangible that would set the orbit of the adoptive child to its gloaming.

As that authority, we assert here that we as children shall not be the last of thoughts when adult-kind holds forth on our welfare. We shall be the beginning of thoughts and the ending centerpiece of thoughts. We hold that the fate of our possibilities shall not find its end beneath the residue of politics, policy, and finance. We will not be the inheritors as children of what older mouths spoke forth as barriers to our emancipation from drift.

Our storm shall be told in poetry and prose. Our thorns shall foretell the coming of our rose. Our every unique cultural truth shall be held in the light of society's scramble toward mature humanism.

We assert the right to have and express struggle with our circumstance without lambaste for daring ingratitude for the blessings of family that befall us. Cannot the ocean bemoan the weight of its belly even as it enjoys the splendor of its majestic bounty? We declare these things as solemn and true.

Our charge too is guided inward. Who goes forth from this uprooted garden should pain to find root in the forgiving earth of relationship. And family will be given a new name. This is our charge and bittersweet legacy. Bound are we by the fickle tether of our fate and who but Turmoil should render forth that river toward peace? The lamp is lit, for always is there a home for the one who would dare believe in Love again.

We are not *the adopted*. It is we of anxious hearts and nimble dreams who do the adopting. And behold us not in language as *adopted*, for that is measure of a past and finished thing. We are more than that legal transaction, that moment of movement across an unsteady stream. No, we ought to be in language called *adoptive,* for our act of bonding with the familial branches of our totality is a vibrant, pulsing thing whose fingers grasp persistently at the fringes of tomorrow. So say we that we are active in this *adoptive-ness,* even into the autumn of our living years.

We are apple seeds planted too shallow in first soil, thus given to the wind to scatter. What seed is designed to thrive in the garden of its unfamiliarity but that bore of higher purpose? Whose choice is it that we germinate and rise? Whose sun bakes us whole even as the hole that bore through us early is caulked and filled with the leaf of loving honor, a leaf that chewed and dissolved, is the healing compound of our ages? Whose sprout left its bed, sleepwalked, resoiled? Who knows the battlefield of nightmares in which our self-Love toiled and threw its mighty blows?

We have tasted the storm at the window, felt the shudder of the pane. Still we remain, nothing so special, and therefore special at that. For we are but every child. And that is the headline of our success. We have been raised, risen, and returned... faithfully to the garden that is our essence, to the orchard of our truth that shaded us from the broil above. To the rock of our spirit's resolve whose wide girth gave us a leaning place.

We have not defaulted the race. We are in the race's mid-water stretch. That place in the ocean before sight of the shore, too far out to have satiation inside, too close to the truth to turn a callous chin.

We are the delta of many rivers, the dusk of many days. We are descendant complexity, spark of perplexity. All manner of mundane, tears of near surrender darting 'tween the rain. We speak mute, our lives explain.

When there is found, like footprints trailing afar, failure by those whose charge is the adoptive child to recognize and resoundingly respond to our particular drumbeat, then unequivocal is our responsibility and right to assert ourselves into that stand of self representation as to our story, nature, need, and chosen mode of existence.

Resolved are we in this, at this season's leading edge, backed against the precipice of misrepresentation. Doubt not that our stand will of need be deeply rooted and that our movement shall be forward toward revelation rather than backward toward misappropriation of our collective potential. Yet we seek the sun. Never in this shall we come undone. The course has been run and now it is the season of the adoptive child to forge into being new stories, documents, and interwoven missions that would so define our spirits' thrust.

This is our declaration, here birthed, and forever to evolve to its living, breathing, and divine potency.

MUTUAL

Do you see me?
If so you seed me,
I take root in you

do you feel me?
if so you feed me

I fill my well with water clean

do you hear me?
if so you heal me

understanding is
the medicine I need

will you be my student?
if so I will teach,
and in teaching
I will learn from you

in marriage, two
make a sacred pledge as one

in this relationship
we cannot be one
without a pledge from two

that you will
seek my magnificence

and I will
seek yours too.

MS. TINA

She
skips rope to the beat
of chocolate milk surging
down a parched
12-year-old throat
in high July

her
bare feet bouncing for relief
off the street,
heart beat moving fleet,
dreams dancing in her head
of when her family will
be whole again...
because she feels:

if
we can just get it
together we'll be okay,
cause we are family,
can't nobody take that away from us,
can they?

that night
in the glow of street light,
hidden under the sheets,
she takes pencil to paper,
feeds her journal these words:

my greatest fears:

she writes,
and as she writes, the words
are also written on the blackboard
inside her mind,
etched on the inner walls
of her heart,
where they will stay,
stubborn graffiti
hidden in the shadows
but persistent all the same

and she writes

my greatest fears:

Mommy dying,
Daddy crying,
bad things under the bed,
somebody taking my family away,
away

I know a way
to keep bad things away,
I'll pray...

I'll do like Ms. Johnson
at the library
when people come at her mean,
I'll look at them scary,
I'll build a wall around my heart,
that way no fires can start
inside my chest
that would escape from
there and burn the rest of me

I'm afraid cause people
don't seem to like my family,
they don't say so with their mouths,
they speak it with their looks,
wish I had me some cookbooks
for all the crooks who
come to steal our joy,
I'd make me up a meal
so hot and spicy
they would have to ask us for water,
least for once they'd be asking *us* for something,
seems like we're always asking
somebody else for something

then they always give us that look,
like we are something less,
and they are something more,
but they don't know my godmother,
she can sing like an angel,
they don't know my
best friend Keisha,
can't nobody add
numbers as fast as she can

they don't know my Uncle Roy,
I've seen him make a gourmet meal
from nothin' but flour and water,
seem like to me

my Daddy, he may not be fancy
but he can dance with Mommy
real sweet and make her feel like
somethin' special when he dips her down

and Mommy, she may not have
all the best dresses and shoes,
she may not talk smart-like,
but she knows more ways to
stretch a dollar than those folks
in suits and nice cars always
stressin' they budget and fussin'
'bout they stocks and *bombs*

and my family,
we sure can tell some stories,
keep you laughin' most the night,
stories 'bout folk we know
and some we don't,
don't wanta know either,
and stories 'bout Moses
and Ms. Harriet Tubman
and Jesse Owens,
stories that make you feel
good about yourself,
yeah we can light a fire
with stories and keep
the house warm 'til
morning light

I just hope nobody ever takes
me away,
cause how would I ever find
my way back,
and why are people always talking
about sending me to a better life,
folk seem awful comfortable
with the idea of me never seeing
my family again

I read my books,
I remember they used to do that
to slave children,
send them away to a better life,
I bet in the Master's house
when trouble came,
the children didn't get sent
to a better life,
seem like folk think children like me
weren't ever supposed to be with
our own families in the first place

yes'm,
I read my books,
they took certain other children away too,
they called it making them civilized,
they used to cut off all their hair,
us, they take us and cut off our memories

but what if I don't want no better life?
what if I just want *my* Mommy
and to play with *my* brother
and keep going to *my* school
and never ever split up with *my* friends?

so what Mommy's not doing well,
I'll go stay with Big Ma,
she Loves me too,
and if not Big Ma,
more than two people in my family Love me,
ain't that true?

I get so tired I just want to sleep
and wake up and us have everything we need,

I don't need another family,
I just want people to stop being so mean to us,
It makes my Daddy cry

Now, that Ms. Tina
from the agency, she for real,
I'll tell you how I know...
most folk don't look me in the eye
when they speak to me,
I mean they do,
but really they just lookin' right past me
like I'm a ghost or something
and they just talkin' to the wind

Ms. Tina she looks me in the eye,
I can feel her gaze settle on my soul,
and when I speak or even when I don't
I can *feel her* listening to me...
now that's some real stuff

yeah, Ms. Tina
she's not like some other folk,
I've even seen her look at Mommy
like Mommy's a real person...
Ms. Tina don't know,
but after she leaves,
Mommy floats around the house
like a queen or something,
I like that cause I don't
think most people see Mommy's beauty,
does being poor make your beauty
invisible?

Ms. Tina she talks to Daddy
like he's a full grown Man,

not a boy...
seem like if you're a man like Daddy
in this world,
if you stand up all the way they beat you down,
and if you crouch down,
they smile and pat your back,
Daddy wasn't made for that I don't think,
but after Ms. Tina leaves I notice Daddy
treats Mommy better,
heck,
he treats us all better

Ms. Tina she don't know that

it must be hard for Ms. Tina
working with all these families like ours,
cause it seems she don't have much support,
some days I see her dragging her spirit around
behind her
like it's about to fall off in the dirt and get lost,
I wonder if a spirit is like an umbilical cord,
wonder if you cut it loose does it shrivel
up and die,
hope I never see that happen with Ms. Tina,
cause then who would treat us right?

and who's gonna believe in us?
I think it must hurt a soul a whole heap
to have the whole world not believe in 'em
except for one person

wonder if that's what Jesus felt like
when they strung him up on the cross...
poor Jesus,
he didn't have no Ms. Tina by his side

sometimes I feel like everybody wants to
crucify our family for being the way we are,
like we did something wrong by not having
money and making mistakes...
don't the people who get to keep their children
make mistakes too?
who's there to scold them?

I remember the time Ms. Tina thought
Ricky and me might have to get put
with another family,
or at least in another home,
I remember how she sat with us
and made us call all the relatives together
to talk and figure out what to do,
I remember how she kept asking
us about our strengths,
I thought she meant who had the most muscles,
later I realized she meant how did we
deal with our troubles

she kept pushin' at us and pushin' at us,
trying to help us help ourselves,
eventually we found a way
for Ricky and me to stay in the family
while Mommy got better,
Auntie Ruth took us in for a while,
but at least my nightmare never came true,
they never took my family away

but you know what?
I do believe that if ever Ms. Tina
had to put Ricky and me in another family,
I do believe she would pick a good one for us,

not any ol' family...
I trust Ms. Tina cause
I think we mean something to her...
most people when they come in our house
they look around and start frownin'

Ms. Tina
she comes in and her eyes always light up
when she sees us,
I don't know if she's just fakin',
far as not likin' what she sees around the house,
cause our house, there's not much in it,
but at least she cares enough about
our feelings to fake like she's happy to see us,
at least she cares enough to act like we mean
something, that's more than we're used to

but Ms. Tina,
I think she really does care...
if I was the people running the agency,
I'd pay her a million dollars
cause that's what she's worth

every time I sleep through the night
and wake up and my nightmare
hasn't come true,
that's when I think Ms. Tina
is worth more than gold

when I grow up
I'm going to make something
with my life,
just so I can turn around
and thank my Mommy and Daddy
and Ms. Tina,

the three big people
who always made me feel like I
was the sunshine
even when the rain was making them wet

Ms. Tina,
I know I don't appear to be friendly
on the surface,
but that's just cause I'm scared
that if I smile
that's where the pain will sneak in
and come back to visit my heart.

she turns the page in her journal
and writes these last words:

my greatest fears:

Mommy dying,
Daddy crying,
bad things under the bed,
somebody taking my family away

p.s.
Ms. Tina:

someday I'm gonna help all the
children just like you do,
you ain't just my hero,
you're my angel too

you take good care of yourself,
I need you to.

12-year-old closes her book,
emerges from under the sheets,
drifts off to sleep
as fireflies mimic the stars...

nightmare chased away for
yet another night.

CHERRY BLOSSOMS

My heart speaks now to you,
the one who would serve to toil
on my behalf

I am the child of your daily labor,
of your nightly dreams,
let me show you something

but wait, I must warn you,
what is to be seen lies this way,
far within my private garden,
in the depths of my treasure chest

come unto me, but come unto me true,
to venture here you must walk naked
and crying, for no cloth must mask your
own frailty,
tears must cleanse you well,
lest you infect my soul,
the very thing you
dare invite yourself beside

I have stories for you,
they begin like this:

you see me small and weak,
yet my spirit is the ocean,
my tide has crept along your shore

I have witnessed your secrets,

you bear them alone and shivering,

your garden has gone cold,
but now is the season in which
you will choose to die or to live

know that this choice is my fate too,
as you die or live, I die or live with you

our spirits are bound as such,
at night you cry out to God,
why have you done this to this poor child?

you do not hear God's response:
*what I have done to this poor child I too
have done to you*

my own cry is different in those same nights,
I cry, *God why have you done this
to the grown ones who toil for me, the child,
that they cannot see my Truth?*

so you see, we are two souls
each crying for the other,
forming rivers of tears that
go ungathered

your garden has gone cold,
the chill wilts my youthful flower

you cry for me, yet your own struggle
steals my sunlight

it is time for you to release your cherry
blossoms and cloud the sky

what then rains down will cleanse your
vision and you will see me true

you will see that as you question
why you do this work,
my child heart questions
why you began this work

whose life you serve in bearing this work,
when will you at last betray this work
and therefore betray me

you will see that though you have
seen me as poor and pitiable,
I am rich and blessed

you see my family roots as rotten,
but fail to see that we are a worthy
tree that feeds on rotten ground

your heart Loves me but your mind
judges me

you see my chocolate skin as
evidence that I come from something
burnt and broken

so you dream for me of places
bright and distant

my roots are not burnt or barren,
only brushed and blemished,
yet firm and fertile,
my family still has beauty left to forge

you despair about my well fare,

I wonder when you will say farewell

stress is a storm sweeping
your valley into dusk,
my future in your hands
is your own sunrise

what you touch in me in winter
becomes my gift to you in June

you fear you make no change in
my life,
but you forget the darkness
you keep from my life

you suffer a starving pocket,
are paid light of coin for your work,
yet are made rich every moment
of this mission,
you look for your payment
in the wrong purse

you spin webs of gold on the fabric
of our childhood futures,
but look for fool's gold in false streams

your heart desires approval for the
battles you fight,
look to your own echo for that,
we create the world in which we live

you wonder how much you can afford
to bleed for me, but
your blood is your own salvation

we eat the fruit of seeds we sow,

child welfare is a harvest of faith,
its true rewards run latent, blossom later
as I grow into the adult who raises
a family like the ones you dream for me

so here we are together,
you wish beauty upon me,
you *are* the beauty upon me

not only have you come to me,
I have come to you,
your work is my ministry,
your Love is my bread,
your endurance my breath,
your desire my warmth

your pain my hope,
your courage my strength,
your tears my drink,
your nightmares my audience,
your faith my shelter

I am your child,
but here in my garden you are *my* child,
I give birth to your glory
every day that I live

now you see me, don't you?
good, because that is why you are here

this is why we bleed,
so that we may send our cherry blossoms
to the sky.

REMEMBERING

An isolated youth dreams of dignity:

I was Africa once,
before the nets and ropes and shackles
and 400-year percolation of spite
that clouded my vision of self

I was Africa and not nearly perfect
but undistorted, rooted, fully human

I was Africa under the palm leaves,
dripping with clean rain,
civilized more *then* than
after *civilization* visited us

I was stronger than the rotting log,
teeming with decay,
weaker than the granite stone
whitening in the salt of bay

I was the blisters on young hands
learning Old Father's deeply oiled drum

I was sure I was human,
I was clear I was beautiful,
I was known, I was seen, I was home

I was all that
before I was this

I am Africa still.

COURAGE

She sat down to write this final note
at midnight on her fourteenth birthday,
using a carving knife to force
the words directly into the oak table...
its flesh gave easily, her courage became words:

I will not fold myself into your genocide,
your killing of the ancestors who live
in the marrow of my yearning bones,
drumming a song you cannot possess...
I am a sun that will not be eclipsed

I will not transcend my heritage,
absolutely nothing is wrong with my heritage,
I reject your demand that I choose
being human over being my roots,
I will be my roots *and* be human,
they are indivisible

I will not transcend my truth,
become soulless flavorless docility
so that you may avoid reconsidering
the long cathedral of your greatness,
you need to transcend your fear of me, transcend
your fear of me, your fear of me, fear of me

night was a kind usher,
its proud arms steadying her as for the last time
she walked out the door of the place where
deeds unspeakable were done

she was become.

DADDY

Maybe it is the full moon
glowing ivory in the indigo sky
that pulls her from her sleep

more likely it is the lifelong hurt
that runs an underground river
through her heart,
soaking her insides with an endless
rain of emptiness

the 10-year-old girl peels back her covers,
sits up,
walks over to the window where
the moon beam illuminates her desk

she sits down there,
taking a pen in her hand,
sliding a few sheets of her favorite
butterfly stationery close

she begins to write:

dear Daddy,
this is the 10th year,
124th month,
3,720th day that I have lived
without you in my life

I know because I count each day
inside my heart

I don't know where you are in this world,
so I fantasize,
sometimes I think maybe you became an
astronaut,
got shot up to the moon,
maybe you're up there now,
the light from your smile shining down on me

oh Daddy,
I wish you were here,
I'm a big girl now and I'm feeling things,
I'm confused

I know you hurt Ma real bad and she hurt you too
but how come I'm the one carrying the blues?
there's a hole where I imagine my peace
should be

I dream of your arms holding me,
that's the only time I sleep peacefully,
and I know you've done some time,
done some crime, slipped and tripped,
but how come I'm the punished one?

I don't get to cuddle to your deep voice,
I wonder, does it sound like thunder?
your eyes are they big like mine?
is your smile wide like mine?
do they call you too, chocolate sunshine?

I wish for things,
I wish I could go for a walk with you,
talk with you,
tell you about my 3,720 days,

wish you could take me to a Bulls game,
or that when I acted in the school play
that you came

wish I could see your face in mine,
wish you could tell me about what to do with
the boys at school,
'specially with this one fool

wish when they ask *who's your Daddy*
that I could show them you,
don't care how you look, how you talk,
how smart you, are what mistakes you've made,
just wish I could show them you

they're talkin' about puttin' me in therapy,
they can save that money,
I don't need no trickery,
I need my hollow spot gone,
I ain't done wrong,
half the music to my song is gone,
I need you Daddy to complete my harmony

I'm confused about things,
I'm feeling alone

maybe if I have me a baby,
maybe if I flirt with that boy Charles,
maybe if I wear my skirt real short,
maybe if I fight with Ma,
maybe if I drink a little, smoke a little,
maybe if I scream real loud...

you'll hear me
all the way out there where you are,
you'll come runnin', find me, see my Truth

my roots are bare and torn from earth,
my reflection pond is stirred up muddy,
I can't see the reflection of you,
the half that completes the whole of me

tomorrow will be day 3,721,
if you don't come, my tears will run

I remember stories of my birth,
Ma gave you 3 weeks to get your act together,
social workers gave you 3 months,
Daddy, now I have to put my foot down

I'm giving you a deadline before I close my heart,
I figure I can give you 30, no, 300, no, 3,000...
okay I'll give you 10,000 days but that's it,
no more

we start counting from,
from,
whenever you say start

I can't help it, I need you in my heart,
don't need no super mom, no fill-in pops,
no shrinks no drugs no grown folk playin' cops

she wrote her final words in bold caps:

I NEED MY DADDY

she got back into bed,
full moon kissed her good night.

SEE ME

Hey, over here...
look over here,
you gotta look hard to see me,
I mean, you see the skin of me, the sin of me,
but you gotta look *deeper*,
I'm not a loser, I'm a keeper

I'm a 15-year-old,
packed with fears but feelin' bold,
emotions cold, heart laced with gold,
I'm a busted up, rusted up,
gonna dust it up, 14-year-old

y'all say I'm troubled, tainted, dysfunctional,
got special needs,
but y'all the ones puttin' boulders on my path,
you say I'm trippin' but I'm trippin' on your stuff:
your anger your fear your prejudice your pain

you say *let's get the boy/girl some intervention*,
but what about your therapy?
cause something is making you blind,
you can't see me,
something is making you deaf, you can't hear me,
something is making you scared,
you won't truly come near me,
something is making you cold, you can't feel me

I act up, you put me on Ritalin,
but I'm just dancing,
grown folks the ones doin' the fiddlin',

y'all play the wrong song, maybe your song,
but not my song,
so I try to step correct, keep getting it wrong

for so long I've wanted to wake up in the morning
and hear *my* song...
you say I put on my tunes and tune out the world,
I'm not tuning you out, I'm tuning *me* in,
trying to find my frequency,
a sound that feels good to me

I'm a 13-year-old switchin' homes,
keep putting my stuff in a trash bag,
I'm tired of being the trash,
I'm not unpacking no more,
not unpacking my baggage,
my pain my pride my people my trust,
see, my attachment tool is starting to rust

you think I'm ungrateful to have a home?
I'm not ungrateful, I'm unsettled

you ever tried to stand still and calm
in an earthquake?
my earth keeps quaking, I'm scared,
but you keep wanting me to bond
so I keep faking, but inside I'm quaking

nobody ever asked me what I want in a family,
they just moved me like I was a dog,
then y'all wonder why I don't act house trained...
I may be cracked and bent but I'm not broken

I have my own ideas about family and
what feels good to me...
deep in the night if I try real hard,

I can find my dreams to
what *I* want in life

don't want no baby mama baby daddy drama,
life already done up and took my mama,
never knew my pops,
got better relations with city cops,
least they come every time I'm in trouble

ever wonder why I keep getting in trouble?
cause cops is my pops
and they spend time with me,
my crew on the street, they spend time with me,
I'm looking for time, not crime,
but seems like crime's the way to get
the time, so I crimes, drop sin like dimes

I'm that 12-year-old you call violent but,
the world is on fire with
your anger and screechin',
I'm just the student of what you're teachin',
I'm not preachin', just reachin' to make sense
of this world

don't get me wrong, I have my dreams,
I'm trying to build my life,
I'm trying to pull fat catfish from
my lake so weary,
but seems like all I keep pullin' is pollution
from my water so dreary...
I'm tryin' to find the sunshine,
life keeps giving me rain

you say pray, have faith,
good things will come today,

but it's hard to pray when my nightmares
keep breakin' in on my day

now, yesterday I had me a vision,
a way to turn my life around

I'm gonna take all the pain
packed away in my chest,
release it to the sky, give it a rest

I'm gonna use it to show my baby sister
how much I've missed her,
see, Pops tried to shoot my mama,
missed her, took out my sister,
now my heart's a blister,
cause Lord I've missed my baby sister

but now I'm gonna turn my pain into paint
and paint me a rainbow,
show the young ones which way to walk,
which way *not* to go

I'm gonna be a teacher a preacher
a healer a reacher,
I'm gonna shine my light, shine it real bright,
you know why?
cause that way maybe you'll have to see me

you'll see I'm a 12, 14, 16, 18-year-old,
a little bruised, a whole lot bold,
so don't pity me, look down at me,
frown at me, grieve me,
best believe me,
I'm gonna shed my skin and shake my sin,
I'm gonna... *make you... see me.*

GETTIN' FREE

Young brothers of every skin,
fronting hard and feeling tender,
heads nodding to the rhythm,
skin bakin' to browns, blacks,
and reds
in the sunlight reflected
off unforgiving concrete
steps

saying *amen* and *that's all right,*
this could be church,
they could be congregation,
this could be a preacher
they listen to
as he feeds them his latest
sermon

except this is not church

in the penitentiary,
during fleeting yard time,
serving for hard crime,
they with their pent up stories,
pushing the peddles that release
their feet,
provide the beat

he,
who could be a preacher,
is a juvenile inmate,

intimates with his brothers,
provides the heat

they tap,
he raps:

I've got tats on my tri's
and yokes on my bi's,
cold in my heart kicks the lights,
peeps your lies

I'm pacing like a caged cougar
on the yard,
liftin plates and pressin hard,

hollerin at my dreams
between the icy bars

dreams are flying away
and out of reach

I'm the bloated fish
washed up on the beach

all these seagulls
pickin at my flesh,
wanna breathe the good air,
can't get none fresh

carrying my water
in a pot made of mesh

aching for my daughter
cause I sold her to the slaughter
and it bought her

now I'm spilling the last
of my salty water

shootin jumpers on the gray,
sun blastin brothers as we play
only game that got us,
look where all this ballin brought us

can't twitch a muscle
without a tussle from the warden
and his system hustle

stepping proper for the Man,
feeling like the lowest,
and not a man

all these *swolled up* brothers
with shrunken brains,
done washed their keys
right down the drains

laughin at the suits,
but now who's wearing
prison regs,
matching jumpers
and matching grills,
passing balloons
powdered from the pills

passing lifetimes making deals,
never getting out,
never getting over

signing on the bottom line,

never reading the finer print,
contracts got us buzzing,
keep us loaded for killing cousins,
dozens die for every six
who see the light

fleets of fireflies
blinded by the night

system shackles on the
left foot

mental shackles on the
right

shuffling around the crowded cage,
family reunion of the slaves

guess we need to bump up
the glory music louder
before we hear the drums
that make us prouder

takes a slick beat
to kick this slickness,
400 trips around this sickness

gotta be the one to slip this track,
gotta get my quickness back

gotta flip the switch
and 'scape this yard,
trying hard but hatred's trying harder

gotta pawn my fears

to make this final barter

long as this nation denies its madness,
it's all on me to climb
the purple mountains majesty

can't be no worse
than dying in the desert
of my thirst
and walking ghostly
on the yard

baby daughter,
I'm coming for ya,
tell all the ones
who wanna keep you
from your daddy,
they can't touch the golden bridge
God has built between us

all the taint ain't enough
to split us
from the heaven
that will admit us
as a baby and her father

I'm going deep inside the slaughter,
mending fences in my heart

a wiser brother schooled me,
said greatness lives within,
I'm signing no more dotted lines,
I already own all a mines

I don't need the Man's release,
just daily praying from humble knees

no more signing hatred's lease,
I own my own piece,
I own my peace

If you can't feel me,
get up off my land,
I'm cleaning up all my
soiled sand

I'm sweeping sacred
spirit from the corners
of my being,
I once was frightful blind,
but now I'm steady seeing

I once did this gig as child,
now I'm going manhood
and bowing down
to lift me up

no more slavin'
on the plantation
of my mind

I'm setting my mentality
ten times past free

I own my own light,
I own my truth,
I own my peace

Peace.

FLEX YOUR X

The dream was crazy

he was 18 and standing before a judge,
courtroom was packed with social workers
lawmakers politicians police probation officers
juvee-heads teachers preachers lawyers therapists
and every foster family he ever had

judge looked down at him and said:

here you stand in judgment
of your *e-mancipation,*
tell the court why you believe
you are prepared to become
a productive member of society

young man took himself a swallow,
stood tall and let his truth be heard:

your honor,
I started out this life as a hummingbird,
just looking for a place to land and,
for whatever reason,
life kept switching up my nest

I did my best to go with the flow,
from this nest to that nest,
after a while my wings needed rest,
I decided that from now on,
I'm gonna flex my X

judge frowned, looking down, and said,
what do you mean flex your X?

young man replied,
X is that thing you pick up every time
a family throws you down

it's that hunger that burns inside
to feel like you belong

it's the way you learn to see past lies
and find the truth

it's the beauty born of a private pact
to prove yourself

y'all see us as nothing more than
train wrecks and rejects,
full of missteps and defects,
but we're a new nation,
we're about to flex our pecs

every day until we *age out* of your system,
we're building dreams inside,
age-ing *into* our life mission,
foster care is a journey of attrition and ambition,
I wouldn't even be alive at 18
if I hadn't lit my own ignition

sometimes I doubt myself
and my fear chases me
with claws and teeth like T-Rex,
but then I remember I was *given* this life
to shape me into something special,
someone who cares about other people's pain

and situations in life

foster care taught me not to give Love pecks
when people need compassion
and their due respects

holding back our Love is what wrecks
the whole human complex

see, X is that factor inside picked up from
the extraordinary foster care ride,
it's about learning how to overcome the hex
and make it your reflex to thrive,
that's how come I'm extraordinary
and I'm still alive

y'all in this courtroom can stop craning your
necks,
we're not rejects with defects,
we're like X-Men,
we've got super-powered reflex

we've been called mutant and outcast,
but we learned what makes each of us special,
our life in foster care is one of those things,
now when life shines its light through our X,
that light reflects on objects lying in our path,
and we have new vision

we step over, we step forward, we rise

we've got a passion y'all can never know,
a passion to set the world straight,
a passion to grow

we've got stories to tell and gifts to give,
we dare to live our lives
in super-powered 3-D,
not like super-ficial cartoons on TV,
we're fully human and full of destiny

so when they treat us like suspects,
we just flex our X,
when they call us derelicts,
we stand tall and represent our reality
like Memorex,
then we use our truth in steps
to rise up over the mountain
and reach our apex,
we keep coming up aces
no matter the decks

when you run your checks on our specs,
you'll find us listed under heroes and she-roes,
because we survived then thrived,
so with all due respects judge sir,
I'm not emancipating or aging out,
I'm stepping in, stepping up,
I'm about to change the game

and to all my people in foster care:
when life gives you mess,
don't stress,
just FLEX YOUR X!

BEYOND THE HYPE

The legislator:

We need to remove barriers to loving homes

The parent:

I Love all my children the same

The child filled with old soul:

We do not honor the One Spirit
of which we are composed
by pretending sameness
but by watering the soil
of our many nations
and feeding that
garden to the

seven
generations
to come

This is Love.

LOOK DEEPER

A child's heart to heart with *the system*:

graciously I ask, did you look for my father
under that rock,
for my uncle under that tree

did you tear up the city
to find my cousin
who might have carried me?

what of my auntie
who used to kiss and cuddle me?

when was it that you met
each and every one of my family,
since you have determined that
none in my family are worthy of me?

why does the
sterility of *normalcy*
mean more than
the richness inside
our family poverty?

why do you value
the norms you bleed
over the things I need?

I like costumes and masks,
but not dressed on the ones charged

with the task of raising me

from them I need
nakedness and honesty,
I need the courage of frailty,
I need to understand
why they keep tripping on me

you say my family had no treasures...
you never opened the treasure chest

you see no beauty in my people
because you cannot *see* my people,
you see only ghosts
clothed in the sheets
of ideas you have been taught

how can you assume people
who scorn what I come from
can make me feel Loved?

a recipe for self-hatred
lives in your philosophy

here is what I pray,
that you don't paint
these challenging words
as troubled, or as whatever
labeling agent used to wash
truth down the drain

I pray that you find
dignity breaking through my pain

can you find a reason
to look deeper at your motives,
your method, your mind?

you may discover that
I am worth more than a contract
that soothes a budget line

some people pay for a child,
but the child is who gets billed,
for lack of consideration
of the difference between
child spirit filled
and
child spirit killed

with all due respect
to the complex
challenge of placing me

I will ask one more time,
did you tear up this world
to find
blood, kin, or otherwise,
the ones who truly
should be mine?

speak truth to me
and we will have a garden
where our imperfections sow
the seeds that grow
to beautiful.

A BETTER LIFE

Heart to heart continues...

Next time, devoted one, could you
find it in your heart
to ask the families who
just wanted to give a child a better life
to list the things they thought
would make my life better

could you ask them to name
the ways they fear me,
fear my people,
fear my fear

how they plan to help me know myself,
how they can help me dry my tear?

How, if they don't know
what I've lost,
can they help me find it again?

do they believe that my past
is part of my better life?

are my traditions part
of my better life?

are my old friends
part of my better life?

can my dreams be part

of my better life?

how about my memories
of what felt good to me?

how about my fitting in?
not sticking out?
having not to shout
to be heard from inside?

I weigh what was
against what is
a thousand times a day

I'm not sure what
better means in your mind,
but I have a feeling
some of my *better* I've left behind

do you mind?

some of my better
is found in today
and what looks to be coming

do you think a singer
would be better if she
had to choose between
notes of her humming,
or a drummer between
beats of his drumming?

I am asking for your help here,
does better start where trouble ends,
or do new troubles mean
that now better begins?

can I miss what I had
and be Loved in the present?

can I live in the future
to manage the ghosts of my past?

and if I miss my family,
and my school can't be family,
and my teams can't be family,
and my friends, teachers, coaches,
neighbors, world can't be family

and if my family can't be family

can I at least choose
in my heart
who gets to be
family to me?

I know I cannot control
the weather or whether
tough times come my way,
I am reminded of this
every moment of day

but can I at least choose
who to let in my heart?

can I choose?

I'm not sure what better is,
but I believe
a choice is a start.

GENTLE BUTTERFLY

It was a tea party with her favorite doll
beneath the cooling pines
in her lemon summer dress...
something on her heart to confess
to her porcelain friend:

You are that gentle butterfly, and I,
I that hand that must remain
a soft and open and freeing place to land

the butterfly I have spoken of so often in the past,
thinking it was I pleading for a hand that did not
grasp or smother my fragile light

the butterfly I sought beneath my bed at night
and on the perches of flowers
in my dreams,
and ran to barefoot across
wet morning grass
when sun was new...
that butterfly was not I,
she was you

you are that gentle butterfly, and I,
I must remain a good and safe
landing place

I will do this for you...

butterfly
and I.

A LETTER FROM THE HEART

The letter was written on sun bleached
paper the frail consistency of old skin,
tucked in her favorite journal, where
her child, as of yesterday a college student
and far away from

home

knew she would find it

she sat on her auburn couch
near the window in morning's
eager light
and read,
a starburst of revelation,
a bundling of years of the unsaid,
a kindling for new Love

she had never encountered
her baby's voice in this
inspired persona

this is what her baby's courage said:

There is no simplicity in relationship, only
moments ripe with potential for joy and pain.
Both sensations may bring us growth. This is a
truth as relevant for parent as for progeny. I
believe a child is a spirit with the strength to
withstand storms on the way toward fulfilling life

purpose, but is also blessed with a delicateness of sensitivity and intense feeling.

What to us in our more tenured years are bland expanses of emotions in reaction to life, are vibrant explosions of waterfall and lava to a child in the midst of raw wonder. Each moment in the experience of family, for a child, carries treasure chests of emotion we can only strive to imagine from our grownup vantage point.

I as a displaced child need things most particular from you. Love, which you may consider as the crowning of my provisions, is, though precious, only the baseline of my sustenance. I am *of Life*, come to you, and by nature I am a social being. I develop myself through my relationship to and experience with other human beings, and with Life itself.

Because of this I need these basic human requirements, which should be written up as human rights, and exercised as our human salvation: I need to feel a sense of connection to you. I need to know that you go beyond the quick and easy step of loving and into the challenging and rich process of respecting all that I am, and may come to be, even to the extent that my truth may discomfort you. I need you to address me with truth and not deception-as-a-means-of-protection.

I need you to understand that my identity, self-esteem, and ability to nourish myself, stem from the health of your identity, self-esteem, and ability to nourish yourself. I need that you not exercise impulses borne of your own insecurities as you raise and nurture me, but that you exercise those impulses in other spaces. So that I may receive from you nurturing derived of a mentor's wisdom—you have come before me on this path.

I need that you spend time working on your understanding of why you chose *me*. To communicate, not only early on and initially, but also enduringly, and in many ways why you chose *this particular manner of embracing particular me*. Do not tell me why you wanted *a* child, but why you want and Love *this* child—me.

Do not expect a child to easily accept her arrival into a new family as being as natural and unquestionable as that through birth; our natural propensity in life is to ask why. Tell me why the sky is blue and tell me why I am a part of you.

Just as all children need constant reminders of their parent's Love, I need consistent validation of *the goodness of my distinctiveness from you*. Not direct redundancy, but varied portrayal of the values you claim to have as reason for wanting me. Let it show up not only in direct conversation, but also in the way you live; the way you relate to certain other people and places and events. Let your living be your proof.

If you do not provide me this, I will answer for myself such questions about my place in your world and this world, and I will answer from the insecurity of my searching. If you do not want society and its strangers to provide my answers, then you be my messenger. Use honesty, and if you are not sure about a thing, then use that opportunity to show me what it means to be human: Tell me that you do not know, but will invest in coming to know. If I know that you have made an effort in regard to an aspect of *Me*, even if it is not directly an aspect of *You*, then I will later in my life know something more of what it means to be *We*.

I need that you remind yourself which of the two of us is the priority when it comes to sacrifice of the ego or comfort. I am tender. You are life-tested. I need you to go about this work with the diligence and frequency that you might give to your own education, work, passions, and other relationships. And then give more. I need you to take the weight of perfection expectations off your shoulders, so that you can stand taller and take deeper breaths as you nurture me with a devoted imperfection. I will remember not your imperfection, but your perfect commitment to my entirety. I need you to reflect, reckon, heal, and grow so that you can shepherd me to my same.

I need for culture to become a reality in your consciousness, like the weather is now, so that you respond to its realities within our family, within yourself, and within me. I need those responses to be humble and fluid as they relate to how you have been socialized through your own cultural experiences.

What you believe and expect for others (especially family) to respect, may not be what I come to believe and need for others (especially you, my family) to respect. I need you to know that my life is to be lived toward the purpose of my blossom. If you have not already reached your blossom, humbling yourself to the integrity, validity, and dignity of my spirit may fertilize your own blossom.

I need for you not to be afraid of me. What sounds absurd is truly at the core of many family relationships. It is the feeling of threat to our sense of validity and worth that flames us toward jealousy, resentment, defensiveness, control, a deaf ear, a blind eye, spite, and power-tripping in our way of relating to a Loved one.

I need for you to accept that the ideas, values, and people that I identify myself with as I grow will surely be influenced by you, but that they will not ultimately be dictated by you. I will remember forever your guiding arms and words, but will spill tears throughout my years in thanks for the freedom that you allowed my spirit, which is by nature a force of freedom.

I need for you to not magnify or obsess over my displacement circumstance, nor my ethnic or other distinctive character. I equally need for you not to ignore, deny, or avoid the same things about me. My characteristics and circumstance are not cartoons to be exaggerated or gawked over, nor are they meant for invisibility or to become *something the family doesn't talk about.*

I am not a tragic drama. Be light with yourself in discovering me. I believe that balance is the key. My truth is like your personality: it is a thing that simply is. And when it is not attended to, appreciated, or respected, not only do I not feel good, but also I am diminished. You who claim to Love me are then tethered to that smothering of the flame, and we all grow cold.

Please do not be misled by the surface decorations of ease and discomfort, for what comes easy to you in dealing with my needs may truly be a spoonful of bad medicine for both of us. And what comes through discomfort as you struggle to do right by me may be the most loving potion you may offer.

I need you not to feel threatened by the people and experiences I have descended from in body and spirit, through the generations of time. Rather, you might relate to these roots of mine as jewels in the treasure chest you acquired in your initial embrace of me. These jewels can be your support as you nurture me, so please do not through insecurity and fear try to separate me from what I have come from, of what I am a part. These things, more so than any nation or manmade thing, are indivisible, and you will only have succeeded in causing disruption within me. You need me to be whole, so that we as a family can be whole. And my intimacy with people and culture not of you and yours is in fact a central ingredient in my intimacy with you and yours.

I need urgently and critically that you find the motivation, reason, courage, and strength to plunder the holds of your soul for the prejudice that we all surely carry, and spend some time with those energies; especially as they relate to social categories into which this world might place me. For, how can you honestly carry prejudice in your heart toward what is a part of me? No manner of costume, makeup, or mask that you may adorn to disguise yourself from me would be powerful enough to stay your prejudices from me. In the end you would only betray yourself in single, forever-lasting words, actions, and energy. And I would always have to carry that painful contradiction of Love living in the place where I should not be confused—in my family.

I am child and so I need. I need. I need. I need. But a secret I can share with you is this: What I need, you also need. I am complex but ever so simple, just as you are. Look for me, truly look for me with sincerity, and you will know what is best for me. I believe in you, in what you have come from, and where you are going. Believe the same of me, and when I grow, whatever pain I may have come through, I will look back upon my life beside you with thankfulness because you nurtured me with a humble imperfection, and set me free. I drink from you. I find comfort beside you. I find myself in you.

You are my reflection pond.

Calm the water's surface for my looking.

COME BE MY EARTH

The student was given a choice
of subjects for the oral presentation...
chose to speak on Nature:

The nature of my roots
is not as decisive
in my life as is the nature
of the earth come to bind with me

earth of relations feed me,
water me, pollute me, poison me,
heal me, strengthen me, hold me,
fail me, become me, shape me

will you spit me out,
soil of my present day?
or take me in,
which requires you mold
yourself intimately
around the shape of my soul

teacher of this moment,
you are all the light
I have been given for
this stretch of road

shine on me,
light my path before me,
reveal what lurks around me
in pregnant shadows

but I beg of you, *be the light,*
be the good earth, a steady bed,
the stronger soil, a richer spot
in fallow ground

come be my earth

my roots are made to respond
to ground that feeds them

stroke my ends so bravely,
and we shall make amends,
I will send my shoots deeper *deeper*

I will become such a tree,
quite the vine,
accomplished flower,
a cause enough for planting

I make good seed,
just wrap me in your courageous
soil poised to learn

find my worth, dirty my husk of seed,
wet the shell, soak my flesh,
coax my downward sprout

my upward is pulled by Sun Above,
downward thrust though
is a rooting *must,*
a fingering through
thick and buried mud

find my worth, bring on my suckle,
be my good and courageous earth.

SEASONS OF CHANGE

Another move, another starting over

a leaf flutters,
a heart joins the dance,
a child begs the world:

I have met the bitter wind,
abrupt end to habit's shelter

kneel with me now
as the mud grows deep and cold,
for I do not know the rate
of my descent
nor whether the ground line
shall rise to consume me

pray thee that I might
be buried but to become a seed
and sprout again,
green and not broken thusly,
yearning again to pierce the crust
and wave with confidence
beneath the sky of a rain retreated

this life,
this piercing life,
sweeps us low,
the plowing,
raises us high,
the harvest

what majestic winds we bear,
what brunt of storm
before the weeping calm
that ushers in new light,
and leaves us:

gasping, spent,
gaping, open,
bridled, bound,

ears to soil,
anticipating
next unanticipated
unyielding sound

wading into waters unknown
begins with a shifting in the heart
long before movement finds our legs

inertia is a beauty we serenade
until it swells and fills our cup,
scales down its castle wall
to settle within us,
the peasant dreaming
of what life is
beyond the moment,
whose ground we have trodden,
the garden whose soil we have leached,
the time whose circles
we have worn bare

move, we say,
to our own stillness...
it does

move

we are brave now,
leaves turn
even as buds stir within
the branch,
eager for showy spring

we will meet that warm
season at its birth,
for now we are motion,
as all things living should be

smile creases the face
of our desire

even as we splash
the puddles of change
into clouds of anxiety,
we are coming clean

even as we strain to
un-become this weary note,
we are learning a new song

a song first sung
by a shifting in the heart.

SUNSHINE AND RAIN

The teacher was moved to tears
as she read the story turned in
for her seventh-grade class
by a boy whose turbulent life
could not dim his promise:

A man led his small boy down the path toward
home. On the way they passed a wheat field
where an older man toiled in the heat. The elder
was revered in the community as someone who
had a deft touch for bringing peace to local
conflicts, and for soothing suffering hearts. The
father cleared his throat and called out, Son, say
hello to this gentleman. He is a great man.

The elder replied, Thank you for your
kind words. However I fear you surpass reality
with your view of me.

But you are such a wise man, the father
replied. You seem to see things others do not. It is
as though you have access to a world beyond this
one.

No, the elder offered. I am not a wise man.
My intellect is simple and my thoughts hard to
come by, I do believe. I am simply a man who
uses his pain well.

This brought wonder across the father's face.
What do you mean you use your pain well?

The elder stood up, straightened his spine,
and looked the father in the eye with a gentle

gaze... A farmer of course cares about his crops, yes?

Yes, of course.

Well, then, what farmer would use only the sunlight that comes to his field but avoid using the rain water that falls, keeping it from his growing harvest?

None, of course.

Yes. None, of course. Then why do you feel that so many souls use only the sunlight of life but run away from the rain of life? You see, the sunlight of life is those pleasant moments and experiences that bring us easy joy and laughter. We don't think twice about rolling around in that hay, celebrating it, making it a part of our personal and family heritage. Those pleasant emotions become the food of our storytelling feast. We reflect on those feelings. Because they feel good to us, we enjoy exploring those feelings for their deeper meaning. You could say that most of us use our happiness well.

I see, said the father, holding his young son by the shoulders, fast at attention. Please continue.

Unfortunately, too many of us run away from the rain of life. The rain of life is the pain of life: The deeply hurtful and difficult feelings that come from our unpleasant experiences. The rain of life is the wounded-ness that comes to us as an unavoidable daily dose. It is part of the parcel of being alive. But we have been taught to take the pain of life as a negative thing, as a thing to avoid at all costs. This is neither accurate nor realistic.

The pain of life is not negative; it is difficult. There is a difference. A negative thing has no potential other than destruction and harm. A difficult thing may be unpleasant, yet its greatest potential is when it is used for something productive and positive.

We cannot ultimately avoid pain. It is sewn into the moments of our being. The rain that falls from the sky may leave us soaked and cold and wishing for the sun, but that very rain is feeding our crop; satisfying our harvest. It brings us just as much chance for good things to happen as does the sun. And yet we run away.

With the pain of life, we talk about how the past is the past, and it's important to move on, to not dwell in darkness and so forth. We have constructed an entire language for our children that teaches them quite stupendously to treat the pain of life as insurmountably negative and something to flee desperately.

The truth is just the opposite. We must teach our children that they may enter straight into their pain, confront it honestly; and with the proper tools they can nurture that pain into some of the most powerful personal characteristics a soul may carry.

Most of all among these is compassion: The capacity and habit of desiring for others that they do not suffer. From a compassionate heart an amazing river may flow forth from any of us. A river born of the work we have done with our pain; a river that is often misinterpreted, as mine is, as wisdom or unearthly insight.

A long moment of silence. Then the father spoke: You have humbled me and opened me all at once. I believe I hear you saying that most of us waste fully one half of what life brings us. That simply by making use of the daily grace of pain, just as we make use of the daily grace of joy, we can see ourselves and each other much more clearly.

The elder's creased face smoothed into a smile. I could not have put it more *wisely* myself. Why not use what we are given? Life gives us joy and pain, and nature is in harmony with this truth by offering the world sunshine and rain. Both bring growth and fruit to the crop of souls. So instead of leaving our pain to rot and fester in the internal bins we construct with our fear, I say sit down with it and learn to know it, for there is sour yeast in even the sweetest of breads.

The father turned his son down the path. Goodbye, Sir, and thank you for this lesson. I see in the clouds that the rain soon comes. I'm going to get my son home.

So that you can avoid the rain?

No, Sir. So that we can gather the rest of the family and go stand out in the rain!

The elder clapped with vigor and grinned his hearty satisfaction. Go, my children. Go and use your pain well, and reap the harvest of a beautiful life!

SING YOUR SONG

Good night, teddy bear...
are you feeling lonely?

tonight I'm going to tell you a story
and sing you a song,
so you can smile while you sleep,
and tomorrow we'll spend the whole
day just listening to each other

I know that makes us both feel better

okay...

Uncle Samuel told me once that people spend
their lives acting foolish because they think who
they are ends where their bodies ends. He said if
we could see ourselves as we truly are, as music
flowing into each other, we would know that we
can't treat each other badly because the whole
world is just like a spider's web, and each of us is
only a strand in that web.

He said our body is meaningful, but that it's the
song in the body that means even more. The song
tells us what we're doing here, and lets us find out
what we mean to each other by singing our song
and listening to everyone else's song. He said our
song is our spirit, and when we call out with it, it
bounces off of everything, even the sky, and

comes back to us. That lets us know where we are in the world and where we need to be.

I guess that makes our song the thing that allows us to know who we are and where we came from. Because if we can hear our own song, I mean, listen real close like, then we can know where it came from, who gave it to us, and where we need to go with it.

Uncle Samuel says people get lost because somehow along the way on their road things happened to separate them from their song, or to make their song become quiet. Like with slavery or poverty or homelessness. Or when somebody treats us bad, or when there is nobody around who understands our song in the first place. Or just when someone tries to choose our song for us.

Here is a song that I have for you:

Oh my teddy,
you're my best friend

you listen to me
even when

I say the same things
over again

about my heart
and now and then

about the dreams
I carry here

to one day cry
a silver tear

and wrap it in
a cloth of Love

and bring it
to my mother dear

so she can
plant it in her garden

and it will grow
from silver tear

to a vine of roses
and mother dear

can finally mend
her longing heart

and see how she
and her baby child

are not so far apart
indeed

see, distance can be
made less hard

when we imagine
the bridge of Love

that spans all miles
and never fails to hold

even when all else
grows cold
and evaporates
like summer snow

I'm a child,
but this I know

spirit is a body
without end

and what was lost
will come again

at least in Love
if not in flesh

and so I smile
in my rest

I know mother
mother dear

is not gone
but warm and near

oh my teddy,
you're my best friend

you listen to me
even when...

and now I kiss you
to your sleep

teddy, teddy,
you're my
best... friend.

I AM A JAZZ NOTE

I am your child,
I am a jazz note,
play me

I am silence,
make music with me

this time I'll be the saxophone reed,
purse your lips,
kiss me... so I soften and bend
to your breath

kiss me

this time I'll be the fingers,
you be the keys,
when I stroke your notes,
surrender to me, to me

our home is an orchestra pit,
an opera house,
the walls are soaked with your song,
now let's play mine too

I want to *hear* me when I wake
in the morning,
I want the sun to rise and warm me,
I want the wind to race through
the house and splash over me,
I want you to greet me with a
freestyle harmony,
you play the base line,

me, I'll do the treble cleft

make my breakfast eggs taste
like hallelujah in my mouth,
seasoned with your sweetness
from this spicy Cajun South

I'll put on my clothes for school,
but I'll still be cold because
my nightmares keep leaving a chill

so drape me in melody:
the stories from your child days,
wrap me in your chorus line:
blended passions that fill your heart

and here's a start:
praise me

even as you hold me,
scold me, mold me, lift me,
pray for me, lead me, show me...
praise me

cause when I leave your house,
our house, I hear music, strange fruit,
I hear songs sung wrong,
I hear flat notes, sharp tones,
broken melodies, hate stained piano keys,
I hear people in the street,
at school, and on TV
singing *at* me, not to me, with me,
but at me, through me

they blue me, scare me,

doubt me, shoo me, they take me,
break me, betray me, scorn me,
pity me, but never see me

they string me, not musically,
but up a tree, where they noose me,
then kick out the base beneath my feet,
they loose me, I swing loosely

I like drawing and sports and movies,
they paint me bland and flawed
and... see... I groove ease-y,
I groove easy

you can plow my field,
hoe my soil,
make valley where I toil,
hurt me with a single raindrop,
cause my ground is baked hard and cracked

I'm not broken,
not a foster plaything token,
my fate just got to smokin',
now I'm hard but hardly broken

some days I catch God's glory rays,
feel like slammin' down crawfish étouffées

other times I'm suckin'
limes and feeling sour,
cause grown folks toss me like a hand grenade,
scared of me but *they* got all the power

some days I'm grinnin' like Satchmo
or scowling like Miles,
maybe I'm bluesy like Louisi-ana in the rain
or just hanging in the mist

with brother John Coltrane

what I'm sayin' is,
I'm not the spot, I'm not the stain,
I'm that tune that takes you,
dances in your brain

find my pain, my joy, my purpose, my song,
sing me, hold me, pray me

scold me, make bold me, hear me, say me,
Luther sang it:
make this house a home,
no more wander, no more roam

you Love me? Good, now see me,
you can't be me, but believe me,
I need you to release me so *I* can be me

so sing me, song me, right me,
cause this world done wrong me

tell me why you think I am the Beauty,
cause life tells me I am the Beast

leave Love letters in my bed,
scatter them like rose petals through the house,
I'll find them, read them,
come to Love myself

I am your child,
I am a jazz note

Play me.

BEAUTY AND BELONGING

The young man,
displaced from his homeland and family,
and now a mentor, delivers his closing
Achievement Ceremony address
to the audience: adolescents completing
a rites of passage program for refugees and
migrant souls no longer fortunate to be judged
in the context of their natural cultural beauty

for they live in a world
that does not know them

therefore they have had
to retreat into the trees
among those who care
so they might rediscover their light

therefore they are here to hear him say:

You were born beautiful. You have always
belonged. All that is required of your life is for
you to spend it discovering your beauty and
realizing that *to which* you belong. You have an
eternal, all-powerful song. If you find it, sing it,
you can't go wrong.

Remember who you are. A descendant should
have a memory of that from which she descends.
Without this memory she is not whole. She is
lost inside the illusion that her life is an

individual journey, a solitary foray. Inside your heart live many ancestors. They will be strong and brave for you.

Congratulations from the place in my heart where hope is found, for your achievements of graduation and transition. Your greatest achievement is not a grade or a diploma. It is the way in which you have shaped your character. How you treat yourself and others will define your life.

I have all faith in you. I pray that you always have the will to shine your light. This world needs your illumination! Be a lantern. Be the way home for a child somewhere.

A young friend once shared with me the name she gave herself. She wrote it in music. Now I write it into you. Your name is...

eternal cause,
rain of ages,
eager vine,
brave sojourn,
daily author,
tango sun,
leaping heart,
deep seer,
waking tide,

your name is... *Beautiful*...

YOU RAISED ME

You raised me...
I was a corn stalk stalked by chaos...
I was supposed to be a towering edifice,
a pyramid, a monument to the sky,
but circumstance broke me down,
I don't know why, but I was crumbled
to grain to dust and dust again,
a sugar cane, soured in the shade,
a cherry tree sapling, bruised by hailstone,
a tender buttercup, my downside up,
and you raised me,
you praised me, you saved me,
you took me to the river
and dipped me down,
you cleansed me, washed me, remade me

you waited for me,
waited for my anger breathe,
waited for my fear to recede,
waited for my trust to sprout,
for my beauty to come out,
you waited for me

you made it for me,
made my daily meal:
two slices of hope,
three laughs easy side over,
a glass of fresh squeezed joy,
and a warm bowl of healing,
high in fiber of nurturing

you helped me sing, you found my thing
lost in the dust that chaos brings

you led me to my song, at first
I sang it wrong, but you sat with me
while I practiced it, soon I grew so strong

I learned my song, I earned my song,
I burned my early notes
in the fire you set for me,
and now I sing from memory

I sing symphony, epiphany, destiny

you lifted me,
you sifted me of all my sin,
you grifted my frown and gave me grin,
you hollowed out a treehouse space
where I could climb the vine of fantasy
and hang out in a crown of tree

from there I look out across Vision Valley
and see all my future majesty...
you lifted me

you prayed with me, you stayed with me
in the midnight hour, with candlelight
and cups of tea

you helped me find my power,
looking out the window at bright full moon,
we found stars together that pointed the way
for what I was given life and breath to say,
what I was born to tell the world,

now my flag unfurled, my rose uncurled,
my voice exposed, my pain transposed
into powerful clarity, I be the sweetest rarity

you walk with me, you talk with me,
you listen when I share,
you show me a thousand silent ways
how much you care

you bring me stories, your childhood allegories,
you bring the monsters out from under the bed
and hold them in your candlelight, so I can see
that monsters have no hold on me

you wake with me,
you flake this stone with me,
this masterpiece I'm steady making,
you're never faking, always forsaking
the easier path, so I can swim in
Truth's hot and healing bath

you shine me up, you line me up
and give me salutations, you honor me

you raised me, you praised me,
you showed me what Love
looks like as it lives inside
a heart, a house, a childhood

I wish you would now take a pause,
and receive this gift I bring to you

I bring you my Sacred life,
lived on Purpose with a light not
conquered by hurtfulness,

I bring you my Sacred life,
evidence of what you poured faithfully

you braised me, in your Loving sun,
your patient Loving hum,
the power of your Loving drum,
you braised me

you raised me, you praised me,
you saved me, you slayed the shadows
and gave me light, you gave me life,
you gave me right, now I ascend,
majestic kite, I know my flight,
I have my target locked in sight:

A lifetime lived in a land called *Beautiful*

I'm on my way, I'll get there soon,
and when you look to pregnant moon,
that smile you see looking back down
will be my Joy, and the light I shine
will simply be reflection of
all you were and are to me

whether we are side by side
or near or far, remember,
I am an always brightening star,
and that once and still,

you raised me.

TITLES AND NOTES

MIRACLE'S FACE 9
October 24, 2012.

I LEAD MYSELF 12
Written for California Youth Connection Leadership and Policy Conference, Thousand Oaks, CA. August 4, 2012.

THIS HOME I AM 17
August 17, 2012.

YOUNG LIFE NEEDS MUSIC 23
Written for Ventura County, CA, Youth Celebration, Camarillo, CA. April 27, 2011.

I CHOOSE TO BE ME 28
Written for California Mental Health Advocates for Children & Youth, and Youth In Mind, Annual Conferences, Pacific Grove, CA. May 4, 2010.

WHEN I OPEN UP MY BOOK 31
Written for Ventura County, CA, College Preparation Youth Symposium, Oxnard, CA. June 3, 2010.

MY HOUR COMES AT LAST 33
Written for Ventura County, CA, Independent Living Program Youth Graduation Ceremony, Ventura, CA. June 4, 2010.

Services, Office of Community Services, Professional Training Seminar, Monroe, LA. March 12, 2004.

REMEMBERING 135
Poem honoring heritage in the context of social removal from origins. October 29, 2006.

COURAGE 136
March 8, 2007.

DADDY 137
April 5, 2005.

SEE ME 141
Written and recited as part of a keynote for the Ramsey County TECHR Conference on social group disparities in Minnesota child welfare and juvenile justice, St. Paul, MN. March 24, 2005.

GETTIN' FREE 145
July 7, 2007.

FLEX YOUR X 151
Written for a keynote for the California Department of Social Services, Foster Teen Forum, Northridge, CA. June 24, 2006.

BEYOND THE HYPE 155
A prior version appeared in *Black Baby White Hands: A View from the Crib*, Jaiya John, 2005, 2002.

LOOK DEEPER 156
December 4, 2007.

A BETTER LIFE 159
December 4, 2007.

Jaiya John was born and raised in New Mexico, and has lived in various locations, including Nepal. He serves his life purpose through the blessings of faith, family, writing, speaking, and supporting young lives. He is the founder of Soul Water Rising, a global human mission.

Eddye "Adiya" created the artwork for the book jacket of *Beautiful*. She is one of the Beautiful ones.

Jacqueline V. Richmond, Charlene R. Maxwell, and Kent W. Mortensen graciously served as editors for *Beautiful*.

Titles available through booksellers everywhere. Revenue from Soul Water Rising titles and speaking services funds our *Young Life Drumbeat* youth development programming.

Other Books by Jaiya John

To learn more about this and other books by Jaiya John, to order discounted bulk quantities, or to learn about Soul Water Rising's global work, please visit us at:

soulwater.org

facebook.com/jaiyajohn

youtube.com/soulwaterrising

twitter.com/jaiyajohn

itunes (jaiya john)